Carquinez
Review

2020

ISBN 978-1-7354999-0-1
Library of Congress Control Number: 2020914350

Published by Benicia Literary Arts
P.O. Box 1903
Benicia, California 94510
www.benicialiteraryarts.org

Benicia Literary Arts, founded in 2012, encourages reading and writing in the community by producing events, creating a community of writers and readers, encouraging their development, and publishing their works of poetry, fiction, and non-fiction.

President, BLA; Project Editor, Carquinez Review: Jim White
Editor-in-Chief, BLA: Mary Eichbauer
Story Editors: Mary Eichbauer, Marty Malin, Lois Request, and Jim White
Cover Photo: Beth Grimm
Book Design: Jan Malin

Printed in the United States of America

~~~~

Carquinez Review

2020

Writings from the
Carquinez Strait
Shoreline Communities

Introduction

On behalf of Benicia Literary Arts, I welcome you to the *second* inaugural edition of *Carquinez Review*. If this book were a ship, it would be on its second sailing, not its maiden voyage. Dave Badtke published the original *Carquinez Review* in 2000. Badtke and his editors created a beautiful book that showcased Benicia and our North Bay region's many talented artists and writers with an eclectic mix of memoir, fiction, poetry, photography, and art. The anthology you now hold in your hands is devoted to the works of regional prose storytellers. We hope that future editions will include other creative expressions.

We like to think of Benicia as a prominent part of the North Bay's cultural establishment. The town is small enough that our literary-minded citizens tend to know one another. It's almost impossible to walk the length of First Street without greeting someone deeply engaged in the literary life. Yet Benicia's artistic and literary influence extends well beyond our beautiful shoreline bordering the famous Carquinez Strait. Our poets and authors, as well as our artists, are familiar names at open mics, in bookstores, and at exhibits throughout the Bay Area. Conversely, we benefit when Solano, Sonoma, and Napa counties increasingly draw leaders in the arts to Benicia's gallery events, readings, and presentations.

Benicia's growing literary and arts reputation is nourished by a vibrant Arts and Culture Commission; the Benicia Public Library, provider of vital services to the community since 1910; Bookshop Benicia, our literary hub; and Benicia Literary Arts, *Carquinez Review's* non-profit publisher.

In the 2000 edition of *Carquinez Review*, Badtke wrote in his introduction, titled "Strait UP," "*Carquinez Review* was created to redress, in a small way, our tendency to discard our stories and art." His sentiment still resonates with us twenty years later. We believe everyone has a story to tell.

So please, read on! We hope you will be inspired to open that desk drawer, revisit *your* stories, and share them with us in future editions.

I want to thank my colleagues at Benicia Literary Arts for sharing my vision to assemble some of the wealth of material we have at our fingertips into an anthology. I hope *Carquinez Review* serves to express something of my enjoyment and gratitude.

Jim W. White
Project Editor
Benicia, California
November 2020

For more information about Benicia Literary Arts,
see our website at www.benicialiteraryarts.org.

Consider joining us!

We exist to support writers and readers, and
we're always seeking new members.

Contents

Reflections

Visions

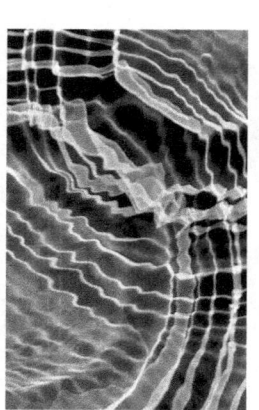

Encounters

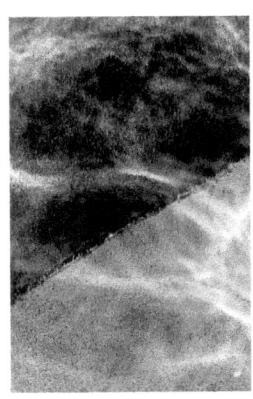

Crossroads

Reflections

~~~~~~

Key to Cherokee

by Teresa Van Woy

*Coming together is a beginning; keeping together
is progress; working together is success.*

—*Henry Ford*

After a long day in the Great Smoky Mountains, Mama
said our visit to Cherokee, North Carolina, would have to
wait till morning. She drove through the small town, then
parked the camper further down the highway next to a fast-mov-
ing river. The next morning, we washed our oatmeal bowls in the
raging water, then Mama drove the eight of us to the Oconaluftee
Indian Village.

We hung out near the camper while she spoke to the person at the
ticket counter, then she came back to give us instructions. "Y'all are
gonna have to pretend you're under twelve," Mama whispered to
us. My brother Leigh rolled his eyes. "Under twelve? Seriously?" He
dragged his heels to the entrance, but went along with it, since his
only other choice would be to wait outside in the sweltering heat.
No one said a word about an eighteen-year-old pretending to be

eleven when he walked in—or a seventeen-year-old, or a fifteen- or fourteen-year-old. Jon Eric and the twins and I were the only ones who didn't have to worry since Jon Eric was twelve, I was ten, and the twins were only five.

A woman, who introduced herself as Ama, began our tour by explaining how her outfit was the traditional way the Cherokee women dressed. She had long black hair pulled back in a single braid to show off her beautiful beaded earrings and necklaces. A brooch, pinned to the top of her dress, was made from bone, and her wraparound skirt from real buckskin leather.

"Leather?" I asked, thinking of Daddy's leather belt he'd some- times whip us with.

"Yes, feel how soft it is."

As she explained the process of smoking deerskin to prevent it from becoming stiff, I dreamt of having a pair of suede moccasin boots like the ones she wore. The kind with pretty turquoise and maroon beads embroidered on the top that matched her earrings.

"Follow me," Ama said. "I'm going to take you back in time to the life of the American tribal people."

We followed her through the village, which was kind of like a museum, but way better. More like a camp with real people show- ing how their ancestors used to live. Ama showed us everything from men hulling canoes, to ladies making pottery from the clay they had collected near the river. Others demonstrated how they wove yarn with their fingers, and how they made baskets, tools, and musical instruments.

Ama had us take a seat to watch a reenactment of the Trail of Tears as she tended to a fire in the middle of a staged area. Soon other Native Americans joined her in dancing, drumming, and chanting near the fire. I chanted along with them in my head, and imagined myself as an Indian girl, dancing around the fire with them, singing and celebrating Mother Earth as they had.

As the show went on, President Andrew Jackson's soldiers rushed into their camp with rifles and bayonets to force them to relocate onto reservations. I imagined myself right there with them in my buckskin dress and long suede boots. I grabbed a blowgun from one of the mud houses and escaped to the hills, leading others from my tribe to safety.

I sank low on the bench after an explosive gunshot brought me back to the reality of the play. I wasn't a hero after all. I wasn't with them in the 1830s to save the day, or dancing around the fire in my buckskin dress. I was just one of the tourists watching as one Indian after another collapsed to the ground on the thousand-mile walk to the reservation.

I cupped my hand over my eyebrows so no one could see the tears form in my eyes as I learned that nearly a third of the Indians died along the way, either by starvation or freezing to death. That's where the name "Trail of Tears" came from.

No one said much after we left the village while all the history sank in. We crammed back in the camper, then Mama parked in a lot near an enormous statue of an Indian chief. We couldn't wait to see this town. The streets were lined with tourist shops, like a lot of other places we saw that summer, only Cherokee was cool because it was on an Indian reservation. Everyone but Jon Eric and I headed into the first shop they saw on the corner. We wanted to explore on our own, so we went across the street to a store that had every fun thing imaginable—miniature teepees, bows and arrows, tomahawks, and pocketknives.

"Hey, check this out," Jon Eric said.

He put on a Daniel Boone hat made of real fur, then pointed a wooden gun at me. "Pow!" A small cork stopper attached to a string flung in my direction.

"That's cool," I said.

I wanted to dress up, too, but in something more Indian-like. I tried on a pair of moccasins, then put on one of the fringed vests, but it still wasn't enough. Then I spotted it. High on a rack near the window, a fancy headdress glowed from the sun shining through its soft white and grey feathers—the type only a chief would wear. Using the bottom shelf as a step, I stood on my tippy-toes and pulled it down. When I put it on, its long feathers reached down my back, almost touching the floor.

I knew it was only there for the tourists because Ama told us the Cherokees never wore those types of headpieces. She said they weren't that fancy. Their tribe only attached a single feather to a patch of long hair they kept on their shaved heads.

I spun around to model my new look, then picked up a small rawhide tom-tom. It reminded me of guys back home in San Francisco who sat on the steps of Aquatic Park playing the bongo drums on the weekends. I lifted my knees, one at a time, and began dancing in a small circle as I banged on the drum.

"Hi-ya, hi-ya, hi-ya, hi-ya," I chanted.

Jon Eric took his hat off, picked up a tomahawk and danced around with me.

"Hi-ya, hi-ya, hi-ya, hi-ya," we both sang.

"Ah-hem!" The shop clerk cleared her throat and cinched her brows tight.

My cheeks burned like the coals of fire at the Indian village as I placed the headdress back on the shelf. I wanted to tell the lady we weren't making fun of her tribe, that we were only having fun, but I was way too embarrassed. She probably wouldn't have believed me, anyway. I kept my gaze to the floor as I followed Jon Eric out the door.

We walked from store to store down the touristy street, still trying on outfits and playing with the souvenirs, but without the chanting, so, now, no one seemed to mind.

"I wish I had money to buy something," I said. "Especially a pocketknife."

The store had all kinds of cool knives, from really expensive ones with turquoise embedded in the handle to some with handles made from real deer antlers. I didn't need that type though. All I needed was one of the tiny cheap ones made from plastic that had "Cherokee" printed on the side. A knife would have been the perfect thing to keep me from being so bored in the camper.

"If I had one of these, I could carve little people out of wood for us to play with," I said. "And make a canoe and stuff like that.

Maybe I should go look for some Coke bottles to trade in."

We went out to search for bottles, but a small arcade caught our eyes instead. It reminded me of Musée Mécanique, a place in San Francisco with old-time, interactive games—only this place had live animals.

"What the heck?" I asked.

In a wooden crate with two plexiglass windows, a white bunny sat near a small red fire engine. "The Rabbit Fire Chief" was painted on a sign above it. We waited to see what would happen when a tourist slid twenty-five cents into the money slot. The quarter dropped, the lights on the truck turned on, and the little bunny hopped to the steering wheel to press a button with its paw. A loud siren sounded as the rabbit stood on its hind legs and pretended to steer the firetruck.

"That's so cool," I said. "I wonder how they taught him to do that?"

We followed the tourist to "the Dancing Chicken," then the "Piano Playing Chicken," and went back and forth, over and over again, as more and more tourists used their quarters to give us free shows.

"I haven't seen any of the other kids or Mom in a while, have you?" Jon Eric asked.

"No. The last time I saw them was a long time ago."

"I guess we should go look for 'em," he said.

We walked from store to store, peeking our heads through the doors, scanning the aisles for our brothers and sisters. Then we went from one end of the block to the next, and from one side of the street to the other, but there weren't any Thompsons anywhere. What started as a relaxed stroll quickly turned to panic.

"You try this side of the street again, and I'll check the other." The words raced from Jon Eric's mouth as he spoke.

Instead of just looking in from the sidewalk like our first go round, we ran up and down each aisle of every store calling out their names, "Mama . . . Gregory . . . Rachael!" Still, no Thompsons. Jon Eric and I met at the end of the block, then ran toward the parking lot where Mama had parked the camper earlier that morning. The huge statue of the Indian blurred as sweat dripped into my eyes, but that didn't stop me from running. We rounded the corner next to the statue and I stopped in my tracks when I didn't see the camper.

"Oh, my gosh! She left us!" I shrieked.

High-pitched sounds came from my breathing. Sounds I had never heard before, as if I had swallowed a whistle, or something. I placed my hand on my chest and hunched over to catch my breath as the sidewalk spun around me. *I think I'm gonna pass out.*

"There's no way, Teresa, she couldn't've left us." Jon Eric looked at me, hunched over and pale faced. "You okay? What's that noise?"

I raised my head when the spinning stopped.

"I'm okay. I don't know what happened."

Jon Eric's big brown eyes darted around the parking lot. "She probably just drove to a grocery store or somethin'. Besides, some-one would've noticed that we weren't there."

It's true. Somebody would've noticed.

"But, even if Mom *did* drive to the grocery store, there's no way she would've taken all the kids with her," I said.

"True. Come on. Let's go check the stores one more time."

We each took a side of the street, and went from store to store, aisle to aisle, calling out their names, but still nothing. We ran back to the parking lot to check for the camper again, then all the way to the Indian Village, stopping only every once in a while, to catch our breath. There wasn't a single sign of a Thompson anywhere.

"Maybe we should tell somebody Mama left us," I said. Tears ran down my cheeks as I found a spot on the hot curb to rest.

"We can't do that. They'll call the cops." Jon Eric inhaled a sharp breath and sat next to me. "Besides, Mom has to realize she left us at some point."

I couldn't believe it. We were left behind. Abandoned in Cherokee, North Carolina. Jon Eric put his hand on my back as my body shuddered from crying.

"That's just great," he said. "What are we gonna do now?"

I didn't have an answer for him. I had no clue what we were going to do. I wanted to come up with ideas, but my mind was too foggy. Even with Jon Eric next to me, I felt alone and scared. I thought back to Officer Mike, and the time I got lost on the 19 Polk bus when I was seven. And how, even though it took a whole day to find our apartment—at least we found it.

"I don't care if they call the cops," I said, hoping he would agree.

Jon Eric stood up and reached his hand out to me. "Come on. Let's at least see if we can find some Coke bottles so we don't starve to death like the Indians did."

My belly had been screaming for food all day, but that was the last thing on my mind now. Especially with my stomach tied in knots. Jon Eric was right, though. We had to eat something. What if Mama never came back for us and we were stranded on the sidewalks outside the Indian stores forever? Or even worse, what if we were put in those wooden cages and had to perform each time someone inserted a quarter in the slot? The thought made me whimper even louder.

Tourists looked on as we scrounged through the garbage cans on each corner of the street. Even the kids, children our own age, saw us. I kept my head down and repeated over and over again, *Don't worry about them. You'll never see 'em again. You'll never see 'em again.* We didn't have a choice. We had to search the garbage cans on the main strip. We couldn't check the cans on a side street because this was where all the tourists were walking around with their sugary soft drinks.

We dug through all sorts of trash—melted ice cream, crumpled papers, empty cigarette packs, even some nasty diapers. Yellow jackets and ants feasted on discarded scraps of food as we rummaged our way through each can. After pulling out a few bottles, we headed to one of the stores that sold candy.

"I bet that lady behind the counter is called Black Hawk since she won't stop watching us like a hawk," I whispered to Jon Eric.

If only she knew about the time when Jon Eric and I stole money off a table in a restaurant to buy Mama a birthday present. And how Mama scribbled Xs on our faces with a permanent magic marker that we couldn't scrub off for days. If the clerk knew that, she would have known we wouldn't be stealing anything from her. We learned that lesson loud and clear.

We picked out a couple of Chick-O-Sticks and two bags of chips, then set them on the counter along with the sticky bottles. Black Hawk had a puzzled look on her face as she rang up our items. She was either grossed out by the dead ants, or thought we stole something. Sure enough, as we reached for the door, she called out to us.

"Hey, you two. Can you come here for a minute?"

Crap. Everybody's gonna think we're thieves. Oh, no! What if Jon Eric did steal somethin'? My heart pounded in my chest as we headed back to the counter.

"Hey, I was wonderin' if y'all could help me with somethin'?" she asked.

She tapped her fingers on her chin while waiting for our reply. I knew the next thing out of her mouth was gonna be for us to turn our pockets inside out.

"Uh . . . sure, what?" I shrugged my shoulders and looked at Jon Eric.

Please don't have anything.

"I'm looking for the Key to Cherokee," she said, tucking her long black hair behind her ear. "Would y'all mind goin' to the shop next door and ask the guy behind the counter if he has it? I'll give you each a quarter if you do that for me."

"Huh? The Key to Cherokee?" I asked.

"Yes." She opened her till, pulled out fifty cents, and placed a quarter into each of our hands.

Embarrassed by the lines of dirt on my palm, I quickly pulled my arm behind my back, squeezing my fingers tight around the coin.

"Okay!" I said.

I looked at Jon and smiled before we ran out the door. At the next shop, the man behind the counter tugged at a turquoise bolo around his neck as he spoke on the phone.

"Huh? Uh-huh. Okay," he said into the receiver.

I couldn't stand still. I put my finger in the ring of a keychain and spun it around as we waited. It wasn't everyday someone handed me a quarter, especially for something so easy. I felt important and couldn't believe that lady trusted us enough to hand over fifty cents. Maybe, instead of Black Hawk, her name was Gentle Feather, or something like that. Jon Eric nudged my arm and frowned for me to stop fidgeting.

"Can I help you?" the guy asked when he hung up the phone.

"Yeah! The lady next door's looking for the Key to Cherokee," I said. "She wants to know if you have it?"

"The Key to Cherokee?" He scratched the side of his head as he looked from me, to Jon, then back to me again.

I wondered what he was thinking as he glanced at us. Did he think we were special because the lady next door trusted us with the Key to Cherokee? Or did he think we were just street urchins like what Mama always says we are?

"No, I'm sorry. I'm not the one who has it," he said. "You might wanna try the next shop over. They may have it there." He fumbled through some coins, then handed us fifty cents to split.

"Thank you!" I said.

I bit on the inside of my lip to try and hide the huge smile on my face. I wanted it to look like we were on official business, and all, but I couldn't. No way. Not with fifty cents in my hand. I couldn't even walk to the door without skipping.

"Oh, my gosh!" I said once we were outside. "I wonder what the Key to Cherokee is for?"

"I don't know, but it must be pretty important for these people to want it so much."

We continued from shop to shop, each time with the same results. No Thompsons, no Key to Cherokee, and an extra quarter in our sweaty hands.

Try next door . . . try the pottery shop . . . here, have an ice-cream cone . . . ask at the Skylift, I think he was the last one to have it . . .

We scarfed our Chick-O-Sticks and chips, then went back to the parking lot by the big Indian statue to see if Mama came back for us. Even with the thrill of our new adventure, the empty lot left a burning sensation in my gut. If she had gone to the grocery store, she would have had plenty of time to return by then. She was gone. She left us. Every feeling under the sun stirred within me—fear and excitement, worry and thrill, hungry, yet sick to my stomach.

"What if Mama never comes back for us?" I asked. The thought triggered the pain in my belly to grow even more intense. "What'll we do?"

"I have no idea! I can't believe she left us." Jon Eric flipped one of his quarters in the air then caught it in his hand. "Come on, let's check the Skylift for the Key," he said.

"I wish I was home right now," I said as more tears rolled down my cheeks.

I watched my feet as they hit the pavement with each step—how my big toe moved around in the hole at the tip of my sneakers. I thought about the river we swam in the night before and how painfully cold it felt. I wished I could be there now—swimming, cooling off. I also wished I had picked a different shirt to wear instead of my favorite one that was way too small for me. Sweat caused it to cling so tight to my body that it made it impossible to take a deep breath. Not only that, the rash on the back of my neck came back. Mama called it a heat rash, but whatever it was, it felt like a thousand hot needles poking into my skin. I wasn't used to that kind of heat anymore. Not since Mama had moved us away from Jacksonville—away from Daddy. But that was a long time ago now. At least it felt like it.

I missed San Francisco, and its cool summer breeze, and the way the fog rolls in over the hills each night—but mostly, I missed Mama. Even with crusty claw marks still on my arm from her fingernails, and even with the painful bruises on my ribs from the last time she kicked me, I still missed her. The twins, too. *I wish they were here.*

"Hey, you two," the operator at the Skylift shouted out as we approached. He acted as if he were expecting us or something. "Can I help you with anything?" He smiled from ear to ear, baring a set of tobacco-stained teeth.

"Yeah, we're looking for the Key to Cherokee," Jon Eric said.

"The Key to Cherokee?" he asked in such an exaggerated way, it sounded as if he were trying out for a part in the school play. He pushed his long black hair over his shoulder and said, "Hmmm, let's see. I'll check."

He looked around the kiosk, lifting magazines, opening drawers, and even dumped out a coffee cup filled with pens, loose coins and other knick-knacks.

"Shoot," he said. "I'm sorry, I don't have it. I'll tell ya what though, how would y'all like a free ride on the chairlift?"

"Really? No way!" Jon nudged me with his elbow and smiled as goosebumps tingled my scalp. I wanted to dance and jump for joy.

"Sure, step right up and I'll get you on the next chair."

Once we were seated, the man pulled down the safety bar and we started the slow ascent to the top of the mountain.

"What's up with this town? I've never met people like this in my whole entire life," I said.

"I know."

The higher we went, the more we could see. From the tree-lined mountains that surrounded the town, to people fishing along the riverbank, and tourists walking in and out of the shops. We could see it all. Even the big Indian statue near the lot where Mama had parked earlier that day.

"I don't see Mom or the camper anywhere," Jon Eric said.

My eyes began to well again. This time, Jon's did, too.

"We have to come up with a plan," he said.

"Maybe we could sleep in the woods and catch fish with our hands, or something," I suggested. "And with the money we earned, we could buy a hatchet and some matches to build a campfire."

"Yeah, but what about that huge black bear we saw in the Smokies?" he asked.

"I got it!" I sat up straight on the wooden chair. "Maybe we could sneak into the Indian village every night and sleep in one of those mud huts!"

"Well, these people aren't gonna keep givin' us money. Especially if we don't find the Key to Cherokee," Jon said. "I guess we could always find more Coke bottles."

When we made it back down to the bottom of the mountain, the lift operator chatted with us a bit before sending us to our next location. He asked our names and where we were from, and stuff like that. When Jon Eric said Florida as I said San Francisco, we had to explain about Mom and Dad's divorce and how we were only together for the summer. I wanted to tell him about the rest of the family—how they were somewhere in the camper and how we were left alone, but Jon squeezed my hand tight as a warning. I don't know why he didn't want to say anything to anybody. That man could probably help us.

"Well, kiddos. You might wanna check the water park," the lift operator said as he pointed to some tube slides in the distance.

"I love Cherokee!" I said. "Y'all are the nicest people in the world here!"

"I think they must know we're lost," Jon Eric said as we walked away. "That's why they're doing all of this for us."

"Oh . . . Yeah. Maybe?"

The water park attendant was no different than anyone else that day. When he didn't have the key, he stepped aside to let us in, and that's where we spent the next few hours. I had so much fun, I barely even remembered that we were left behind until I spotted the camper from the top of the slides.

"Oh my gosh! There's the camper!" I shouted. "Mom!" I screamed. "Mama!"

"She can't hear you," Jon Eric said. "Let's hurry and get down!"

The smell of chlorine filled my nose for one last time as I shot down the slide. We grabbed our shoes and took off running out the gate, then continued down the street in our sopping wet clothes.

"Mom! Mom! Stop!" We shouted at the top of our lungs.

The camper was a few blocks away, but the back door was open with one of my brothers standing on the rim of the tailgate. He must have seen us, because he began waving one of his arms back and forth.

The camper stopped, then made a U-turn in the middle of the street and sped back in our direction. Mama came to a screeching halt next to us.

"Where in the goddamn hell have you two been?" she shouted.

We stood on the scorching hot pavement shifting our bare feet back and forth while water dripped down our legs.

"You left us!" I said.

"I didn't leave you anywhere! You knew we were gonna be parked at that same spot by the river where we were last night."

"We didn't know that," Jon Eric said. "And how would we even know where that is, anyway?"

"It was only a couple miles down the highway. All you had to do was follow the road by the river."

"Yeah, but we had no idea you'd be there," I said.

"What do you think, I'd drive away and leave my own children behind?" she asked.

"Well, that's what you did," Jon Eric answered.

"Get in! I don't want to hear another peep from your filthy rotten mouths."

We climbed in the camper and told everyone of our adventures with the mysterious Key to Cherokee—the Skylift ride, the free ice cream, the fun water park, and all of the quarters we earned. No one wanted to hear about it, though. They didn't want to know we were having fun while they were stuck cleaning out the camper, especially since Mama threw one of her big fits.

~~~~~

We never did find the Key to Cherokee that day, and never learned what it was for, or even if such a key ever existed in the first place. All I know is that town came together as a community, offered us the key to their city, and kept us safe and secure until we found Mama. Perhaps the souls of those who lost their lives on the Trail of Tears came back to protect us. Maybe they keep an eye on their ancestral homeland and protect all those who love and treasure it? I don't know.

~~~~~

Paris Twists Through My Soul

by Grant Cooke

*If you are lucky enough to have lived in Paris as a young
man, then wherever you go for the rest of your life,
it stays with you, for Paris is a moveable feast.*

—*Ernest Hemingway*

S mell can be transporting. Unknowingly, the slightest whiff
can trigger an onrush of memories at the most curious of
times. Instantly the consciousness is transported to another
time, another reality.

It happened to me one Sunday afternoon in a cozy pub off
London's High Street in Hampstead Village. My wife and I, with
our daughter and her husband, had strolled through a quaint and
picturesque London neighborhood. One of the city's most expensive areas, Hampstead Village reminds me of New York City's
Upper West Side, with its tree-lined sidewalks, quirky restaurants
and well-heeled denizens. Telly actors, rock stars like Madonna,
and other celebs, whose trashy habits are the stuff of London's
marvelously lurid newspapers, live around the way.

Kenwood House, a great Regency home, perches on a hill above High Street. The magnificent poet John Keats has a museum here. In one of history's great ironies, Karl Marx, Communism's philosophical father, is buried in Highgate cemetery, close to the park, or heath.

It was a lovely day in London—the rain had stopped, clouds scuttled north to Scotland. The noon sun cast a soft lacy glow over Hampstead's ornate brick buildings and tree-lined walks. High Street was jammed with strollers; it was a prosperous and young crowd, glad to be seen, all smiles and good bonhomie as they mingled and wandered among boutiques and gourmet food shops.

We ambled down twisted narrow paths and then on a side street that led to the two-hundred-year-old pub. It was a classic English pub, all dark mahogany and ornate wood accents, with a large U-shaped bar manned by young gents pulling pints and chatting brightly with the customers. Sunshine enlivened the interior, and we sat at a large table amid several families. It was clear that the pub was much loved by the locals, and it served a proper Sunday roast. Three of us split the chicken and vegetables, but my wife ordered French onion soup, which the pub proclaimed a specialty.

We had whiskies first, followed by a good bottle of New Zealand sauvignon blanc. The food arrived, a wonderfully roasted chicken and a large brown bowl with thick tannish Gruyere cheese still bubbling on top. My wife popped the cheese with her spoon and the sweet smell of caramelized onions cooked in rich ox bone broth overwhelmed me, triggering decades-old memories.

We had a wonderful lunch that Sunday in Hampstead—good food, delicious wine, warm conversation with intelligent, thoughtful young people planning a rich and happy life. Yet, as I did my best to hold up my end, a part of me was off, awash in childhood memories of my French mother, with her stories of survival during one of history's most horrific wars, followed by nights of celebrating Paris's miraculous survival.

When February's thick, swirling fog and deep chill engulfed the little San Joaquin Valley farm town where I was raised, Mom would set about making onion soup. I guess February's dank oppressiveness pushed her usually buoyant spirit back to the sadness of the war and the dead. The onion soup was her tonic, its thick broth a magical transport back to liberated Paris, and those happy nights when only French was heard on the Champs-Élysées.

You see, in the fall of 1944, after the Allies had taken back the city, Paris was impoverished, forced to deeply ration food, goods, and supplies. But they did have champagne, and music, and gallant American officers who were brave and handsome in their pressed khakis, with broad shoulders, trim waists, and a victor's swagger. What the body lacked in protein, the soul made up in gratitude for being alive.

As Mom deftly cut the big rings of white onion that would go into the butter and garlic to cook down and sweeten, she would tell bits and pieces about her life in wartime France. It was not easy to be a teenage girl with dead parents, trying to survive in a world gone mad.

When she added red wine and ox bone broth to the soup and the smells intensified, the stories would take a turn for the happier, and her smile would brighten at the memories of the sheer joy that she and dad—her dashing American lieutenant—had known after the Liberation.

When the jazz ended and the clubs closed, celebrants poured onto the boulevards. As the thinnest of dawn's rays peeked over Montmartre and glanced off the spire of Notre Dame, Mom and her lieutenant would stroll arm-in-arm past the Louvre and along the Seine. Tired from dancing and happy to be free and together, the two young lovers would turn north on rue Montorgueil, into the cacophony of Les Halles, Paris's huge central market.

Cast in an inky light from dirty kerosene lanterns, the market was in full swing, with its narrow trails winding through bustling kiosks. The sharp, pungent smell of heavy garlic garlands hanging from wooden pegs filled the air. Short, barrel-chested men wearing berets and dirty leather aprons pushed handcarts filled with animal parts, yelling to make way. While fish and beef were scarce, mutton and Provencal steak—horsemeat—could be had.

Old women dressed in black with creased faces and sad eyes that had borne witness to too much tragedy watched over mounds of onions, potatoes, beans, and turnips. Fishermen hawked oysters and shrimp. Huge wheels of cheese and a few buckets of butter were available, but very dear. But good French baguettes and rounds of coarse bread were appearing as the bakers of Paris uncovered their hidden caches of flour.

At the far side of the market a vendor made onion soup in large kettles. It was cheap and rich, and it was served with a thick layer of cheese roasted to a golden brown. With bread and a bottle of red wine, it was the perfect feast after a night of dancing and celebrating the miracle that they, unlike so many others, had escaped death, or worse—the Gestapo.

My mother was barely 16 when her father was murdered, and she and her younger brother fled as the Germans descended on Paris in 1940. Four long years later, when Eisenhower, with Patton's muscle, agreed that Major General Philippe Leclerc and the 2nd French Armored Division would lead the Allies back into Paris, she was among the thousands to return.

As a young lieutenant, my father was thrown into the Battle of the Bulge, the last stand of Adolph Hitler's army. For six miserable weeks, from December 16, 1944, to January 25, 1945, battle-fatigued American troops fought 30 German divisions in the densely wooded Ardennes forest. Freezing rain, thick fog, deep snow drifts, and record-breaking low temperatures brutalized the GIs. The heavy German tanks—Panzers— came crashing through the trees, followed by the pulsing barrage of machine gun fire. Smoke, chaos, and death enveloped the forest. The GIs dug in, but the Panzers were formidable, and the Germans ferocious in close combat.

Victory was hard won, and it was the GIs' bloodiest battle, with over 100,000 dead. My father was one of the lucky ones to survive—the Germans were targeting battle officers. When he finished recuperating in the English hospital, he was assigned to Eisenhower's staff in Paris. Not long after, he met Mom.

~~~~~

The Parisians were giddy to reclaim the most beautiful city on earth, with its wide, shaded boulevards, stunning architecture, and outdoor cafés where civilization could be discussed and life experienced. They wore the beret again, played the accordion, and danced at the *bal musette*. But mostly they clung to their Paris, with its glories and its vistas—the Champs-Élysées, the Place de la Concorde, and the Place des Vosges. Hovering over it all was the sharp spire of Notre Dame, for what was Paris without its center? For sheer beauty, Paris had no rival, and by divine providence it had been spared the torch.

"We endured so much," my mother said. "When Paris was liberated, it was like being reborn."

~~~~~

Paris twists through my soul. Unlike the demanding California farm country of my youth, Paris is where my soul seeks the nourishment of ephemeral wisps of beauty and flights of emotional succor that only the City of Lights can yield.

Blood and DNA bind me to it. The gray-green waters of the Seine wash through me. The city's history runs deep inside me, with its centuries of beauty and bloodshed, followed by survival, redemption, and, finally, enduring love. Aching to overcome war, my father, in the middle of the halcyon days of a liberated Paris, met and married my mother, who, like Paris, had miraculously survived.

My parents' story is one of an endless chain of heroic love stories that have marked the boulevards, parks, and byways of Paris over the centuries. Those stories are ingrained in this magical city; they resonate deep within her character and are part of her texture, as surely as her waters flow to the Atlantic.

Parisians have damped down their lust for politics and commerce, modifying it to living well, with style, grace, and a disdain for others not able to grasp the perfection of strolling across the Pont Neuf on a spring morning.

Look closely and you will see Paris as a haughty beauty, her high narrow boots emphasizing her graceful figure. She pauses, lost in thought, over a coffee at a sidewalk café near where the Seine picks up speed as it flows under Pont Neuf. Tucked around her neck, the perfect Hermès scarf draped just so, the expectant tension of adventure sparkling in round hazel eyes. Notice the high cheekbones that drove Picasso to make Françoise Gilot his muse. See the pouty expression that haunted Napoleon until he wed Joséphine. Look closely at the tousled chestnut-brown hair and her undeterred eyes that say, unless you are Parisian, you cannot understand life.

The Pont Neuf connects the Left Bank to the Île de la Cité, the city's medieval heart. Half a kilometer away, across the island, the bridge resumes and connects to the Right Bank. Separated by the island, the green water of the Seine surges, then flattens as it rejoins on its endless journey, as poet Guillaume Apollinaire described it in "Le Pont Mirabeau."

Behind the bridge, the sun bounces off the limestone of Notre Dame, the 13th-century Gothic cathedral that dominates the Île de la Cité. Notre Dame, with its twin towers, leering gargoyles, and exquisite flying buttresses, houses the Crown of Thorns, a fragment of the True Cross, and one of the Holy Nails. Its famous bells toil, greeting the morning, calling the faithful to mass. Notre Dame is Paris's center, and the church beckons to the city's 20 arrondissements that spiral out in a clockwise fashion.

~~~~~

Fifty thousand years ago, a huge 30-foot sheet of ice covered Europe and extended east through Russia to the Bering Sea. As it withdrew, a majestic river was carved from the rocky soil of France. Rising at Source-Seine in northeastern France, it gains girth and flows steadily toward Le Havre on the English Channel. About midway, the mighty river veers west, separates at a rocky promontory, and then rejoins, leaving a flat island in the middle.

Ten thousand years ago, ancient Mesolithic tribes camped on the promontory overlooking the island, spearing the river's salmon and hunting game in the forests. Eventually, the Celts came and drove the ancients out, and, around 250 B.C., a Celtic group called Parisii established a fishing village. The Parisii prospered on the rich lands, and the promontory was a strategic place to control river traffic and commerce.

At the height of Caesar's northern expansion, the Romans came. By the time of Christ's birth, Paris was thriving under Roman rule. Roman engineers planned her streets, built her sewers, and laid the framework for this magnificent city. Two hundred years later, St. Denis brought Christianity to Paris.

As the movement swelled, the Romans captured Denis and two companions. The Roman soldiers dragged the men up the hill overlooking Paris toward the spot of execution. Legend says that, after his execution, Denis picked up his head and walked down the hill, finally dropping at the site of the 13th-century Basilica St. Denis. The martyr's spirit hovers over Paris to this day.

The highest point of Paris, the hill became known as Mons Martis, or hill of the martyrs, eventually just Montmartre. Centuries later, as atonement for the 19th-century Commune uprising, a glorious church, the Basilica of the Sacred Heart of Paris, or just Sacré-Coeur, was constructed at the top of the hill. The view overlooking the city is spectacular and inspiring, and it draws people from the ends of the earth.

Creativity pulses through Montmartre's cafés and narrow streets. During the 1870s and 1880s, Impressionism ruled the Parisian art world. Renoir, Degas, Monet, Pissarro, and Manet were quick to violate the rules of academic painting. Realistic scenes of modern life with vibrant, fresh colors brought new vitality to painting. The artists were drawn to Montmartre, a once sleepy farm village coming alive with new ideas, adventurers, and indulgences.

Montmartre became the center of Paris's Belle Époque, several decades of peace and prosperity before World War I. The era was marked by the celebrations leading up to the 1889 World's Fair in Paris, and was renowned for extraordinary advances in science, technology, philosophy, and art. The great Impressionists were overrun by a new group of wild geniuses led by Henri de Toulouse-Lautrec, Henri Rousseau, Paul Gauguin, and Vincent van Gogh. These young lions painted in richer, deeper colors and were hell bent to leave their own mark on Parisian art. The Belle Époque brought the Moulin Rouge to the world as well as the French phrase *"joie de vivre,"* or joy of living, a particularly ironic phrase considering the horrors brought by the world wars that followed.

But that came later, and Montmartre in the 1880s was the heart of Parisian art. Suffering terribly from stunted limbs and deep alcoholism, Toulouse-Lautrec painted the redheaded laundress Carmen Gaudin, and later the lithe and graceful Jane Avril.

These artists' muses were women of the streets and thin, high cheek-boned models, their inspiration fueled by cheap wine and absinthe. In a swirl of creative frenzy, they pushed art to its limits, making these narrow winding streets come to life as a renaissance of painting erupted. Their passions fueled some of the greatest art ever painted.

After the turn of the 20th century, a young impoverished Spaniard came to Montmartre. Short with dark hair and intense black eyes, Pablo Picasso was so poor at first that gaunt figures haunted his paintings. Picasso's genius emerged quickly in Paris, helped by the commanding personage of Gertrude Stein and her brother's network of art sellers.

While Paris nurtured the painters who created a vision that may never be surpassed, the city also gave the world some of its finest literature.

Where shall we begin? Ah, *oui, bien sûr,* at Shakespeare & Company on la Rive Gauche, near Saint-Michel and Odéon. It is unlikely that our young woman with the hazel eyes and the chestnut brown hair, whom we left lingering over her coffee and lost in thought at the sidewalk café near Pont Neuf, would venture to Montmartre—she being thoroughly sophisticated. However, she knows the Shakespeare & Company bookstore, having bought a thin second-hand copy of Charles Baudelaire's *Les Fleurs du Mal* when she was 14 and experimenting with pale make up and black nail polish.

Later, she upgraded. Giving her younger sister her skinny black jeans and long-sleeved tops, she now favors Hermès scarves, exquisite silk blouses and butter-soft and delicately cut Italian leather coats. Once, she returned to the bookstore, but skipped Baudelaire and retrieved a volume by Nina Cassian, the Romanian sensationalist.

In 1919, Sylvia Beach, a Baltimore expatriate, came to Paris, and, with a little family money and a love of books, opened Shakespeare & Company. With a gracious smile and generous heart, Beach was anchor to a revolving group of brilliant young American and British writers who migrated to Paris after World War I, mostly because it was cheap, and, of course, because it was Paris.

Beach nurtured the wild young men, loaning books and money, letting them sleep in the storage room when wives or lovers threw them out. She advanced the work of Erza Pound and his modernist aesthetic and nearly went bankrupt publishing the first editions of James Joyce's *Ulysses.* She knew Gertrude Stein and Ford Maddox Ford, and helped countless other young writers like D.H. Lawrence, Henry Miller, Ernest Hemingway, and T.S Eliot.

Just as the brilliant young painters of Montmartre came to Paris to make their mark, so the young literary lions did. They settled in the Quartier Latin on the left bank since it was cheap and near the jazz clubs. Just as the painters had, the young writers pushed hard against all boundaries. Henry Miller and Anaïs Nin shocked the world by skating on the edge of pornography, celebrating sensuality and tearing away at the residue of social convention. The strikingly handsome and overwhelmingly successful Scott Fitzgerald overran the Parisian literary scene, while his wife Zelda taught the world the meaning of "flapper." In the end, it was Hemingway who captured the era with his first novel, *The Sun also Rises* (1926).

These brilliant young writers, most of whom were not French, nonetheless embraced Paris. Literature, like science and philosophy, has always found a willing mistress in Paris. She harbors dreamers with poetry at their core, with an extraordinary story to tell. My love of French literature started young when I discovered Alexandre Dumas' *The Count of Monte Cristo* in our small farm-town library. I read it twice, letting the magnificent story of Edmond Dantès—with its themes of justice, vengeance, mercy, and forgiveness—settle into my being. Though Dumas was my first, the other French greats like Voltaire, Victor Hugo, Gustave Flaubert, and Charles Baudelaire became friends over the years.

Along the way, I came across Charles Dickens. Though he was a Londoner, Charles Dickens brought the epic, and tragic, story of the French Revolution alive with his *Tale of Two Cities*.

Dickens' story begins with, "It was the best of times; it was the worst of times…" This surely was the truth of the French Revolution and so much of the nation's military and political history. One cannot write about Paris without commenting on its political history.

The 1789 rebellion of the Parisians citizens, or *"sans culottes"* (literally those without fancy breeches), against the isolated, ineffectual monarchy, changed France and Europe's history forever. Against a Europe dominated by failing monarchies, the cry from the barricades of "Liberté, égalité, fraternité" reverberated, igniting passionate hopes for democracy. A new French Republic with its Rights of Man was born, creating a historic ideal. It was a wondrous time, when the boundaries between the social classes dissolved, and the citizen could stand equal to a nobleman.

Yet, it was not to last. Tragically, Maximilien Robespierre, the leader and philosophical genius of the Revolution, slipped into madness. That which started out so gloriously spiraled into slaughter and darkness. Thousands of French nobility died, and, hundreds of years later, the Reign of Terror still haunts the Place de la Concorde where the guillotine stood.

The overwhelming irony of the Revolution is the beautiful majestic boulevards that crisscross Paris and make the city truly inspiring. After the Revolution and the failure of the First Republic, Louis-Napoleon Bonaparte, the nephew of Napoleon I, came to rule France. First, he was elected as the president of the French Second Republic, then, after a coup d'état, took the throne as Emperor of the Second French Empire.

Determined to rule without challenge, Napoleon III crushed any opposition and set a plan in motion for a major reconstruction of Paris. The intent was to remove the threat of rebellion from those who would construct barricades that clogged the city's narrow streets and brought the government to its knees. He brought in Baron Georges Haussmann to re-plan the city. Haussmann, a brilliant architect and engineer, set about his work with ruthless abandon, tearing out huge swaths of homes and apartments and creating wide boulevards that crossed Paris, making it impossible to restrict the Emperor's horsemen. As ruthless as he was, Haussmann also had an architect's eye for beauty; he created grand squares and beautiful parks and built the Palais Garnier to house the Paris Opera.

Modern Paris with its Avenue des Champs-Élysées and other majestic boulevards, its grand squares and open public spaces to let citizens enjoy its beauty, was created by Napoleon III and Haussmann out of the need to maintain political power, clean up the overflowing cemeteries of Paris, and allow Napoleon III to leave his mark.

In 21st-century Paris, huge economic and social challenges face the city and the French nation—unemployment is stubbornly high and generous social benefits are staggering the nation's treasury. Excessive taxation has taken away the incentive to develop new commerce, and the world's venture capital ignores France and heads to England and Asia.

Yet, all that is elsewhere this fine spring morning. The clouds have cleared and the sun bounces like silver thread among the Seine's jade green waters. The trees in the Bois de Boulogne are budding, their delicate green leaves embracing their moment of eternity. In the Quartier Latin, the pungent aroma of North African spices from rue de la Harpe's Algerian restaurants mixes with the smell of warm bread from the patisserie on the corner. Over at the Musée d'Orsay, the long-dead Impressionists live on among the subtle colors of the water lilies and the brilliance of yellow sunflowers.

At the Shakespeare & Company bookstore, the friendly girl behind the counter smiles and says, "*bonjour*" to a young American graduate student dressed in a worn corduroy jacket, faded jeans, and rough boots. He comes from Montana's hill country, and Paris is unlike anything he has ever seen.

He nods and mumbles "*ça va?*" in return, but is too shy to ask her name, though he has visited the bookstore each day this week. He smiles again and makes his way up the narrow, twisting staircase with its tattered carpet to the section that has used American books.

From the middle shelf, he takes out a ragged copy of Hemingway's *The Sun Also Rises* and settles into the sagging armchair by the window. He will be left alone all morning to capture something very special about Paris, though he doesn't know just what yet. Before he opens the book and starts the tale of the "*génération perdue,*" as Gertrude Stein dubbed it, he glances out the window.

At the sidewalk café near the bridge across the river, sits a chic young Parisian beauty. She adjusts the Hermès scarf and tugs at her leather jacket. Reaching into a large purse, she takes out lipstick and adds a subtle crimson touch. For a moment, she twists a bit of chestnut brown hair, and there's the slightest pout as her hazel eyes glance at her watch. This woman is not used to waiting, and soon she will rise and vanish.

The moment comes, but as she stands to leave, a sleek black Audi comes to a fast stop. The window comes down and a handsome man dressed in a dark suit leans across the seat. He calls her name. She frowns her displeasure, and the pout intensifies. Then he says something, and a dazzling smile replaces the pout. As she slides into the seat next to him, the sun glistens off her chestnut hair.

The day is vibrant. An old fisherman in a tattered sweater and fading blue beret stands on the riverbank with his pole, searching the water with a practiced gaze. The girl with the chestnut hair leans over and kisses the driver soundly. He kisses her back, and the car disappears into traffic.

The American student in the sagging chair on the second floor of Shakespeare & Company smiles at the little drama. The potential of the day seems limitless, and, before turning back to his book, he watches as the Seine's green water disappears under the bridge, on its timeless journey to the sea.

The sun washes Notre Dame white. The Spitting Gargoyle, Stryga, sits on his perch high above the city. Strong hands with big knuckles cup his bored expression as he stares towards the Eiffel Tower. A shaft of light peeks around the cathedral's spire, glances off his wings, and shines on the stony face. His big hollow eyes with their promise of eternity seem to blink.

After all, it is a bright spring morning in Paris that will never come again. The city sparkles: exquisite, enchanting, and beautiful.

~~~~~~~

Great Grandpa and the Recliners

by Beth Grimm

*This is one of a collection of several stories about my
father. They are written for my grandchildren.
By renaming him "Great Grandpa,"
I could almost tolerate his farcical behavior.*

Kids, there are many stories in our family and lots around
Great Grandpa. His "collections" were his friends. A walk
through his house was a cluttered tour into the past. The
furniture and furnishings were almost new to the home when
he purchased it. The décor was perhaps ahead of its time in the
late eighties, but severely dated by the new millennium. You may
be reading this story before he's gone, but it might not appear in
print until after he has passed away. I wanted to get this written
before he headed for the big recliner in the sky.

Great Grandpa was a "collector" of many things. And he never
got rid of anything. He said he wanted his home turned into a
museum when he died. There was some interesting memorabilia
from his Navy experience in World War II and many antiques, as
well as lots of miscellaneous stuff. Most of it was meaningful only

to him and no one else, like his hundreds of golf balls, golf shoes (new and old), baseball caps, visors, matchbooks, swizzle sticks, cheap paperback books, and mugs.

My siblings and I tried to be agreeable, especially in the later years. We all lived several states away and each visited once or twice a year. Getting along with him was a real challenge. My sister and I often suggested things to make him more comfortable, but he resisted.

He purchased the model home on the thirteenth hole of the Pinnacles Country Club Golf Course in the Ozarks area of Arkansas in 1988. Because it was a model home it came fully decorated. After the developer moved on, Great Grandpa moved in. He never got any new furniture in forty years. He just added a lot of stuff.

When he was in his eighties, I suggested a recliner lift chair. I had noticed that he was having trouble getting out of his old rocking recliner. Two blue ribbed cloth recliners had come with the house. Over the years they faded and aged, like Great Grandpa. "Broken in" is what he said…about the chairs. "Really old" is what I thought.

Eventually the footrest brackets broke. So they sloped off to the side if raised. It didn't really matter because there was a gigantic glass coffee table in the middle of the sunken living room that blocked the footrests. There was no more legroom between a chair and the big round table than between the seats in a small puddle-jumper of an airplane. The table held stacks full of books, memorabilia, miscellaneous trinkets, and joke gifts he had received over the years, leaving no room for a mug of coffee or bottle of water.

Great Grandpa's chair fit his body like a glove, a very old, well-worn glove. The seat well was so deep he had to rock back and forth and brace his arms to gain enough oomph to propel himself up and out. The chairs were eventually fortified with seat and back pillows.

In my role as "Miss Dutiful Daughter," I thought Great Grandpa would benefit from a lift chair so I offered to get him one for his eightieth birthday. He said, "No, my chair is 'broken in.'" He wasn't in the habit of saying things to be gracious, but rather, to be right, it had to be his idea. I knew with a little patience, he would come around. He was having a heck of a time getting out of that chair.

I brought it up a few more times as he approached ninety. Getting out of his chair was becoming a real production. I could see it coming. Planted hands on the arms of the chair, feet flat on the floor, rock back hard, rock forward hard, one more back and whoosh, up and out he'd shoot. Sometimes it seemed he would not be able to stop. I could see him toppling over onto the big round table one day. But I'd let it go.

Until the next visit. I know I should've given it up. Every "no" contained a bite, as if I was insulting him.

Sometimes he'd get defensive. "If I get one of these chairs you want me to, I'd miss the exercise from getting in and out of my chair. And this chair swivels too. I can reach everything I need."

"Okay, okay, I get it," I would say. And he'd be happy taking that as an apology.

At some point, just over ninety, he finally decided he'd like a lift chair. I could see the caregiver ladies were having a hard time pulling him out of his chair. The weaker one had to resort to putting a strap under his arms. The sturdier one, Marlen, just "man-lifted" him out. At this point, it was well past simple help and he did not like either method, nor did he want me to see him lifted up with a strap.

He had Marlen, a strong-willed Hispanic woman of about fifty, take him shopping for a new chair. They went to The Recliner Store in Rogers, a place nearby that I had mentioned years before to her and him when I first brought the topic up.

All I know from Marlen's broken English recounting over the phone is that they got asked to leave the store…by the manager. I could make out that it didn't take long before Great Grandpa turned on the young salesman, who was polite, but trying too hard to sell him something he didn't really need. Great Grandpa could appear very affable to strangers, while using a berating tone. It was confusing to them, but clear to those close to him. I could easily envision him accusing the poor young man of something awful, when all he was doing was struggling for the right words to appease Great Grandpa.

Marlen, I could tell from her tone, was mortified at being led out of the store with an offensive geriatric in tow.

But leave it to Great Grandpa. He still had to win. He wasn't home two days when he decided he did want that recliner lift chair he'd tried out in the store. He demanded that Marlen take him back to The Recliner Store. He wouldn't go to any other store.

I know this because Great Grandpa told me a few days later on the phone that Marlen was being unreasonable. I said, "Let me talk to her."

She told me her exact words, "No, Mister Bill. I not go back to that store!"

I was on her side. I said, "Give the phone back to dad," and I suggested no one go back to the store. Instead, I said, "Just have whoever is there this weekend call the store and buy the one you want over the phone, and have it delivered."

The other caregiver did that and he soon had the new chair. He sat in it a few days and then decided he didn't like it.

"Call the store and have them take it back," he ordered Marlen.

"No, Mister Bill, it your problem."

This must've fried him. But he called and was immediately referred to the store manager. He said again they must come get the chair. He didn't want it.

I learned later from Marlen that "they want to charge delivery and restocking fee. Mister Bill would have no of it. He got angry and next day they come to take the chair. Charge nada."

A month later, Great Grandpa finally got desperate, needing a chair that he could get out of without being lifted up. He also liked the idea of a chair with a setting to flatten out so he could do his physical therapy exercises. Like the zero-gravity recliner I had first recommended. But he left that last part out. It really did have to be his idea. No credit to be doled out, for me or for Marlen.

He told anyone that would listen, even me who lived two thousand miles away, that he had to go back to The Recliner Store. He said begrudgingly, "Marlen won't be involved."

I still supported Marlen. "Just ask someone else," I said when he complained. "And try to be nice this time if you can get someone to take you." My sympathy had bailed.

She was one of the best and longest lasting caregivers he had because she could stand up to him and ignore his rantings. Great Grandpa was having trouble getting caregivers. He had a reputation at the agency for being difficult.

And it didn't matter how much wheedling he did, Marlen refused to get involved in a chair quest. Great Grandpa was not about to go to a different store. She was just as stubborn. They reached an impasse.

Sometime within about six months of this chair foray, my sister Barbara and her husband Mark visited Great Grandpa. He said, "Take me to The Recliner Store. There is a chair I want to buy. Barbara knew the history because she and I had talked about this. She didn't want to take him to the store. But the weekend caregiver Elmer was with Great Grandpa. He had been a good friend.

Barbara called me, afraid they'd refuse to sell him a recliner. I said, "Why don't the four of you go. Try to make a party out of it. There's safety in numbers. The store is in the business of selling recliners. What do you have to lose? No one knows you in Rogers. And they won't turn down good old-fashioned money, even if it was from a grumpy old man."

They all piled into cars and went to The Recliner Store. They did make it a game, trying out different chairs and making up stories around Papa Bear choosing chairs. Great Grandpa laughed too, according to my sister, but probably to appease Elmer who was also his former Karaoke buddy. I suspect he was secretly seething at the store manager, since I'd never seen him let go of any grudge.

Somehow in this masked gaiety he ended up with three new recliners: a rocking recliner on a pedestal for him so it would swivel like the old one; a matching rocking recliner for guests; and a ze-ro-gravity lift recliner for his sunroom so he could lie out flat, nap, and do his physical therapy exercises.

I thought it was time to put this subject to rest. Between his in-surance company and me and my siblings, he had not paid a dime and had three brand-new functional chairs. But the very next time I came for a visit and admired the new chairs, he started to grum-ble that he really hadn't wanted new chairs. He said he wanted to sit in his old chair. No rise out of me.

"Your old chair is right over there in the dining room. Want me to move it back so you can sit in it?"

"Well no," and abruptly shifting gears, "I want this new chair. I like it."

Still no rise from me. Finally, he caught on that I was not going to argue or protest, just keep agreeing with him. That just about drove him crazy, so he needed to convince me there was still some reason to feel sympathetic.

"About those chairs over there, would you believe the store manager had the nerve to tell me I'd have to pay a fee to have them take the old chairs and dispose of them? Those chairs are still worth money and they should be paying me for letting them go."

Again, no comment from me, although I bit my tongue. I re-ally wanted to say, "You must be goofy in the head to think they should pay you for those old chairs."

But I was happy. I would be going home soon and didn't have to look at the chairs for long. And I had a comfortable chair to sit in while there.

And now that there were five recliners in the house, I figured my siblings and I and Marlen could all have a recliner party in Great Grandpa's honor while he was looking down on us someday from his big recliner in the sky!

~~~~~~

Cotton Candy

By Tamar Enoch

Maybe it was 1967. I must have been around eight years old. We were at the Douglas County Fair, my parents, my sister and brother and I, late in the afternoon at the end of a Kansas summer. We strolled around the fairgrounds, looking at the booths and the animals. Our feet stirred up puffs of tawny feather-soft dust. The muggy air smelled of sizzling grease, fresh cut hay, farm animals and manure.

Maybe my parents bought us hot dogs with ketchup, mustard and sweet pickle relish for dinner. I begged my parents for some cotton candy, but of course I was refused. All that sugar would give me a cavity, my mother scolded.

Maybe we stopped to listen to a busker or to watch a magician or a clown. We probably rode the merry-go-round. We probably rode the Ferris Wheel. I begged again for cotton candy. My mother refused again. My sister and brother almost certainly laughed.

The day was ending, the colors becoming shadowed. It was almost time to go home. My parents told us we could pick one more ride before we left. My sister and brother wanted to ride the airplanes. The airplanes were suspended by chains from what looked like a giant steel umbrella, and once the ride started, they whizzed in a circle as they gathered speed. At the ride's apex, the chains tilted upward, rising to become almost parallel to the ground. I asked my parents if I could have cotton candy instead. A miracle happened. My mother said yes.

My father took me to the cotton candy stand while my mother bought tickets for the airplane ride. I watched, fascinated as the vendor spun a big mound of cotton candy onto a stick. The deep hard lines of his dust powdered face softened into a grin as he handed over my treat.

To have my very own cloud on a stick in my hand was a dream come true. I walked back to the airplane ride with my father, clutching my marvelous treasure in one hand, burrowing my other hand in my father's large warm grip. We arrived just in time to see my sister and brother scramble aboard a little silvery plane with blue stripes. The operator clanged the gate shut and the ride began. My siblings flashed past in their airplane. I gobbled mouthful, after sticky ethereal mouthful, of pink sweetness. The sun was setting, the sky was streaked with clouds the same color as the mystical mass in front of me. Again and again, I proclaimed my joy. I was so glad I had chosen the cotton candy over the airplanes.

It got darker. The daytime colors vanished as the last streaks of sunset faded above us. My siblings spun past in their airplane, holding hands and squealing, waving at us each time they swooped past.

And then, all of a sudden, all that was left of my colossal mound of sweetness was a slight bit of sticky fluff. A final mouthful, and the sunset-colored cumulus of spun sugar was no more. I gazed at the naked wooden dowel in my hand in disbelief. A cloud should last forever and ever—how could it be gone? And to add insult to injury, my brother and sister were still soaring above me in their silvery airplane.

I began to weep, huge bitter sobs of heartbreak. How could it be that my cotton candy had lasted less time than the airplane ride? Round and round my siblings went, and with each turn, my sobs grew louder. Night had fallen. The lights of the fairground sparkled and blurred through my tears.

It wasn't fair that my treat was over while my siblings were still in flight. We had all been offered the same choices, and clearly, I had chosen the inferior option. I was like the contestant on Let's Make a Deal who gave up the living room set and the all-expenses-paid vacation to Hawaii behind Door #1 for the goat behind Door #2. At first, I didn't understand the contestant's distress. Personally, I preferred the cuddly goat to a room full of boring furniture. But I recognized she had made a terrible mistake when the audience moaned in chorus and Monty Hall clucked in faux sympathy.

At last, the airplane ride ended. My sister and brother clamored over to us, wind-blown and exhilarated. I sniffled as we headed back to our car, squeezing into the back seat between my sister and brother. All the way home they boasted gleefully about how much better their adventure had been than my stupid old candy. I sat between them, marinating in sticky despair. Two roads diverged in the wood, and I—I chose the cotton candy. No one is ever going to write a poem about that.

That wasn't the end of it though. A few days later, I heard my mother recounting her version of the incident to a room full of grown-ups after a dinner party. I stood eavesdropping just outside the door, as I often did, listening to my mother's voice rise with excitement as she captured the attention of the room with my tale of woe.

I turned away from the hearty laughter that followed, my body tingling with inexplicable shame. I knew I had done something very wrong, but I wasn't exactly sure what it was. The light around me changed in a mysterious way, as if the hallway where I stood had drifted into the path of a solar eclipse. Objects kept their forms and colors, but were gloomy in a way that was ineffable because there was nothing bright in comparison.

"Now you see what happens when you do something different!" an angry voice hissed in my ear. *"How dare you ask for cotton candy instead of riding the airplanes? Do you see what happens when you make your*

own plan instead of just going along with the rest of the family? All that cotton candy did was trick you, and now everyone, EVERYONE knows how stupid you are!"

It was Mara, worming her way into my innocent child's heart.

Mara, according to Buddhist legend, reigns over the kingdom of delusion, springing into action whenever it looks like human beings might be on the verge of escaping their suffering. On the final night before full enlightenment, the Buddha spent hours battling Mara, who took on every seductive and terrifying form imaginable. At dawn, Mara fell in defeat and the Buddha awoke, gazing in serenity at the morning star.

Screw you! I say to Mara, fifty years later. I am curled up in my favorite corner on the couch, writing my daily pages. *Get the hell out of my childhood!*

I toss my notebook aside and flee through the sliding doors onto the balcony. The horizon is tinged with the beginnings of dawn. I stretch my arms high and my spine long, rising up on my tiptoes, making myself as big as I can, doing what I have been told to do should I ever encounter a mountain lion. My activated muscles tingle, my diaphragm expands, my lungs fill with long, fresh breaths of morning air. A cool breeze rustles the leaves of the trees around me into a round of decorous applause.

Like a bright wet pebble emerging from thick sand at the ocean's edge, the long-ago afternoon at the Douglas County Fair begins to glimmer from the deep recesses of memory. For a moment, I am back there, my feet tickled by the soft dust, looking up at my brother and sister, whizzing past in their airplane. There are my parents, standing nearby—wait a minute, could they be holding hands?

I can't say for sure, I am too enthralled by the cotton candy on the stick I am holding in front of me. It's my very own cloud, the sweet magic I chose instead of the noisy, scary airplane ride, a cloud just like the soft, flushed wisps floating above me in the twilight sky.

~~~~~

November 21, 1979, Was Just Not My Day

by Frances Fields

On this day, our embassy in Islamabad, Pakistan, was burned down with us inside. The day began as a perfectly glorious morning, as were all the other fall days in Islamabad. I had been so surprised and happy when we went to our new home on our arrival in February. Across the street, we had the most beautiful view of the Margala Hills, with the snow-capped Himalayas in the distance.

Now, ten months later, winter would be here soon, but the day before Thanksgiving was warm and sunny. The turkey thawed on the drain board, not really recommended, but I've always done it that way. We were having a crowd over for turkey and trimmings the next day and I wanted to be sure I could get the bird in the oven first thing the next morning. This is Pakistan, folks, they don't even celebrate Thanksgiving here, but we do, no matter what remote post we're in.

We were off to work and school as usual a bit before 8am—kids to the school bus and my diplomat husband, Dave, and I in the ambulance to the Embassy. I was the Embassy nurse. We drove the ambulance home in the evening in case there was an emergency after work hours. Thank God there weren't too many of those. One example of an after-hours event is the evening when we were called to the Embassy Compound for an injury.

Some of the guys were playing basketball when one of them, Jim, broke his ankle. We were called over to assess the situation. My husband, the Counselor for Administration, normally went along on an incident such as this, as his job was supervisory to any event regarding the staff. We hustled over to the basketball court at the Embassy compound. The ankle had a very odd twist to it, meaning it was probably broken. There was a stretcher in the ambulance, so the guys loaded Jim onto it and into the ambulance. We drove over to the local hospital for an X-ray and a consult with a local osteopath. The doc took the patient to the OR to set the fracture and cast it. This was just the start of a long recovery both here and back home. When Jim decided that he wasn't healing fast enough, he asked to be med-evacuated to an American military hospital in Germany. From there he was sent back to Washington, DC. People serving abroad in the Foreign Service are often very apprehensive and fearful of the care they're receiving. We all feel better at home with the care system we know. Jim never did come back to post, as his tour of duty was up, and he was transferred elsewhere. That was just one evening in the life of the Embassy nurse and her husband.

The Embassy was located a few miles away on a large compound with Chancery building, apartments, club, ball fields, swimming pool, marine house, and other service buildings, as well as about 30 apartments—all red brick as is the Embassy building itself. My husband's office was in the Chancery and my health unit was in one of the repurposed ground-floor apartments. The Health Unit and staff were under the supervision of the Administrative Section, not the Political Section, which carries on the work of diplomacy with the host nation. This apartment had been remodeled in the shape of a medical office: waiting room, exam rooms, offices, and so on.

Lal, the sweeper, was there before anyone, getting the place ship-shape for the day. My secretary and right-hand man, Mr. Malik, was always on time. He was a tall good-looking Pakistani man about 50 years old. He usually wore a brown sport coat. I think he dyed his hair because it was an unnatural golden-red color. A lot of Pakistani men and women dye their hair, especially as it starts to turn grey. And they all seem to use this same color. Maybe it's henna.

The Regional Medical Officer, Dr. Paul Wise, was traveling that week, maybe to Kabul or Delhi. My associate Brigit, another nurse, who was Swedish and spoke fluent Pashto, was also in that day. Pashto is spoken in Pakistan and Afghanistan and was really helpful to us in communicating with some of the local employees from the northern areas of the country. Brigit had lived in Pakistan many years with her husband doing missionary work.

Our morning progressed as usual, with patients stopping by for meds or for appointments or to have blood pressure checks, lab draws, or other medical needs. The office was calm and peaceful, as I remember. We completed our regular tasks and thought about lunch.

At noon, I went up to the Chancery where the cafeteria was located. I loved the dal and naan bread that were on the menu every day. Very spicy, but sooo good. I had my lunch and, before heading back to the health unit, I went upstairs to say "hi" to hubby.

While I was in the hall, a friend, the Cultural Affairs Officer, called me into his office to see buses barreling down the road towards the Embassy from the direction of the University. Pakistani buses are brightly colored, with flags and banners flying from them, and usually people hanging out of the windows. Today these buses even had passengers on the roof. Usually, there were few buses on this road, not packed and without people on the top and hanging out the windows. This was our first warning that all was not well. Before long, people were directed to head towards the vault on the third floor, as the front gates of the Embassy had been broached. None of us really knew what was happening yet, but someone called out that a Marine had been shot.

Steve had been on the roof with other Marines lobbing tear gas at the attackers. This was when one of the rioters shot him in the head. Running, my heart pounding, I headed up to the roof where Gunny and other Marines were carrying Steve into the building. We took him to the vault, a secure area, where, unbeknown to us at the time, we would all shelter in place for the next seven hours.

We were all scared to death. We started to smell smoke and knew the building was on fire. I was trying to keep Steve alive, but his wounds were so severe—the back of his head was missing—that it was a losing battle. I applied compresses to try to staunch the bleeding and gave him oxygen, but he needed a surgical team to save him.

For some odd reason the rioters didn't cut phone lines to the building, so I kept in touch with the local hospital. They were ready for us if we could get there. We couldn't go anywhere. The building was surrounded by angry mobs and it was on fire. We weren't prepared for such a medical emergency in the vault, really not for any emergency of this kind. There was no water and no facilities for saving a life. After more than two hours, Steve died in my arms. I still get choked up thinking about it. Tears flow even after 40 years.

Marcia Gauger, a Time magazine correspondent at the Embassy on business, was trapped with us. Her article on the events of that day appeared in *Time* magazine, December 3, 1979.

Ninety of us waited in the noisy vault. The communications specialists were shredding documents in preparation for evacuating the building. The equipment noise left me with tinnitus, which I still have to this day. Sometimes when I pay attention to it, I remember the vault—the air was smoky from the fire and full of tear gas used by the Marines in the hallway to fend off the terrorists. Because it was difficult to breathe, I got some bottles of water that were used to clean the equipment and found some cloth to tear up. We moistened the rags and held them over our noses and mouths, which helped a little. I still can't believe that some of us who were smokers had to have a few puffs, even in those conditions. What an addiction.

I always thought we would get out of there. It's like you know it's not your turn. I guess, too, we were so jacked up by the whole situation. There was a lot of adrenalin flowing. For me, being the nurse, I felt like I still had to take care of everyone, and it gave me a purpose.

Rioters banged on the escape hatch on the roof. Helicopters flew over. The noise was deafening.

We found out later that the helicopters were the Pakistani military trying to chase the terrorists off the roof. As dusk fell, the noise lessened, and the officers in charge determined we could try to escape. It was almost unbearably hot in the vault, and rubber-soled shoes were sticking to the floor.

We couldn't go out through the hall and down the stairs, as the fire was too fierce. We had to climb up a ladder and out through the escape hatch. We crossed the roof and down the other side away from the fire. Someone had propped bike racks up against the building and that's how we climbed down to the ground. Some of the women were crying and saying they couldn't climb down and I remember saying, "Then move aside so others can go!"

The red glare from the fire and the smoke were surreal. Finally, we made it down and into the vans the Pakistani military had waiting for us. Last to leave was the Marine Sergeant with his dead Marine, Steve, over his shoulder. We were then taken to the British Embassy a short distance away. After tea and scotch, and talking to our children on the phone, we left there to go to our own homes.

During this time, our children were at the International School of Islamabad, several miles away. We were in phone contact with the school during the afternoon and learned that there were rioters there as well, but that the guards had chased them off with baseball bats and broomsticks. We worried about our kids; we were relieved that they didn't have to suffer the fire and terror that we were seeing—and happy to hear that parents had picked them up and taken them to the houses where adults were at home.

Normally, they would go on the school bus, but because we feared that the rioters would attack their buses, we made the decision to pick the kids up in private cars. Cars, I might add, that did not have the diplomatic plates assigned to the Americans. The kids had been scared for us when they'd been told what was going on, but were also told when we were safe.

Much later that evening, somehow or other, we all got to bed amid plans for what we would be doing in the days to come. We knew we'd have to be evacuated. But to where and when? The next morning, amid prep of Thanksgiving dinner, we heard that we'd be evacuated the next day back to Washington, DC. Dave and other essential personnel would remain to carry on the business of running the Embassy. Regardless of the burning of the Embassy, the job of diplomacy had to continue.

USAID had their offices in a building close to the Embassy compound, and that's where they set up the new Chancery. The burned-out compound had to be cleared and plans for a new struc- ture developed. Not only was the Embassy itself burned, but the apartments, employees' personal cars, and the motor pool vehicles were destroyed. There was a lot to do in Islamabad and they didn't need women and children there to worry about. And, who knew, rioters might attack again. In the end, the Pakistani government paid for the rebuilding. I've never been back to see that, but the kids and I did go back in September the next year for a short time.

Thanksgiving dinner was a bit rowdy, as I remember. Lots of drinking going on. Who could blame us? We were all nervous about further terror and the long trip home.

A Pan Am 747 had been turned around from a flight that had ended in New Delhi and commandeered to take us back to the States. We were taken to the airport, accompanied by armed guards in police/military vehicles. No one bothered us, and we left Islamabad without incident.

We had to fly to Lahore and Karachi, Pakistan, to pick up people from our consulates in both those cities. Then off to an Army base in Frankfurt, Germany, for refueling and a chance to get off the plane for a few minutes. And some made straight for the bar. This was the longest damn flight I'd ever been on. Everyone was going stir crazy. To make it worse, knowing that we had lots of people on board that didn't know when to stop with the drinks, I'd asked the flight attendants not to serve alcohol. I didn't need to be dealing with a bunch of drunks and people throwing up or falling down.

I was still the nurse and was responsible for their care till we got home. I had a bag full of first aid equipment and medications. I splinted the forearm of one of the kids who'd hurt himself at the school running into the kitchen to hide when the rioters were approaching. He later had an X-ray and casting when we got to DC. Many people—all, I'll bet—were anxious, and some asked me for tranquilizers, which I gave out sparingly. The flight crew was really good to us; imagine their job that day! I think we were en route 24 hours or so.

We were all thankful and excited to arrive at Dulles International Airport in Virginia. We were greeted by many friends and relatives. It must have been at night, but they came anyway. There were tears and lots of hugs and laughter. We were met by our good friends Kay and Dick, whom we'd served with in Ouagadougou, Burkina Faso, West Africa. They were living in Alexandria, Virginia, and came to the airport to see us. We were so happy to see them.

All the evacuees were taken to a hotel in DC and asked to keep a low profile before being debriefed at the State Department. This was scary! A security person wrote down everything I had to say about the situation. Because of the Iran hostage crisis at the same time and the delayed action by the Pakistani government to save us, there was fear that loose lips might sink ships. After all, our spouses and other employees were still in Islamabad.

It took several days to process all the paperwork needed to get us back to our hometowns. airplane reservations, pay vouchers, medical clearances, and all the rigmarole attendant to Big Government. Someone loaned us a VW bug to get around in. I remember the kids piling in like proverbial sardines. We visited friends and went to the Mall, where huge TVs were playing the news of the hostage situation in Iran. I was mesmerized by the footage, while the kids ran around like wild things. Most of them hadn't been Stateside for many months. Somehow, the kids, mostly high-schoolers, were able to figure out how to get t-shirts printed up to mark our adventure. The shirts said, "NOVEMBER 21, 1979, WAS JUST NOT MY DAY."

This November, on the 21st, it will be forty-one years. It was time for me to write something about that day. My memories of Pakistan are good mixed with bad. It is a beautiful country with a rich culture and marvelous cuisine, the people warm, friendly, and colorful. Traveling to the high country of Hunza and Gilgit, our pilot made a sharp left turn into the valley below, just about grazing a magnificent mountain, part of that memorable time.

Shy

by Nancy Freeman

My first-grade teacher, Mrs. Swan, wore old-lady black lace-up shoes with thick heels. I know, because in the car on the way to back-to-school night my mom said sternly over the backseat, "Speak to your teacher! Don't just look down!" But all I could muster was to hang my head and look at her shoes, and I was scolded all the way home. Whenever we were on our way to see grownups, Mom would bark, "Speak to them!" These three words struck terror in my heart. At recess one day, Henry crowed, "You're bashful! I'm gonna call you Bashful!" The cringe-worthy nickname stuck for about a week, and I just wanted to die.

The year before, in kindergarten, some of us tots were crawling on the floor when I accidentally kneeled on a thumbtack. My knee hurt like crazy and was bleeding, but I was too shy to call attention to myself. I tried to become invisible and held my hand over the wound, but a girl noticed and ran to the teacher who put on a band-aid. At home, Mom was annoyed that I hadn't spoken up.

The San Francisco Chronicle held a weekly art contest for kids with a prize of two dollars. I entered a drawing of a family in a car and titled it "A Ride in the Country." To my delight, I won, and my art was in the newspaper. What I wasn't counting on was that my second-grade teacher, Miss Fairbanks, would bring a copy to class and ask me to stand up in front and tell them about my drawing. Crimson with shame, hot and shaky, all I could do was gaze down at my desk and mumble, "no." Bruce eagerly leapt up and did the show-and-tell for me. I was so grateful.

Now and then my dad would bring home a tape recorder from the school where he taught. My younger sister, without a trace of self-consciousness, would sing, make funny noises and tell stories while I steadfastly refused to utter a word. I knew my parents were disappointed, but they never forced me to perform. I wished I could just have fun with it, but I was paralyzed.

When I was six we moved to a new house. I was out in the front yard when a boy about my age came by and said, "I'm going to Karen's. Do you want to come?" I thought to myself, *Karen…I've never heard that name. I wonder who that is.* My hesitation prompted him to shout, "Well, do ya or don't ya?" Startled, I ran into the house in tears, and the boy and I never did become friends. Karen turned out to be a loudmouth know-it-all and had nothing to do with me.

Sometimes after church our family would watch Liberace on TV. I was totally enthralled with this flamboyant genius and begged and begged for a piano till they relented. I took lessons and wasn't half bad. Eventually it was time for a recital. I panicked. I'd have to play in front of an audience? "Noooo, don't make me do it!" I whimpered. Dad praised my performance of "Dance of the Frost Elves" and assured me that if I practiced a lot it would all go smoothly, not to worry, because I was so talented. Then he added, "They'll like it so much they might demand an encore!" When he told me what that meant, my terror was compounded. He tried to diffuse my fear by saying that each child would play only one piece and that he was just joking about an encore. Not convinced, I learned a second song just in case. When the dreaded day came, I agonized through "Frost Elves" without incident, and was vastly relieved when it was over.

A few years ago I came across a stack of my report cards. Every teacher without exception made the same comment: my school-work was fine, but I never participated in class discussions. Not much has changed!

On the first day of fifth grade Mrs. Smith went around the room and had us tell our name and what hobbies we enjoyed. Adrenaline flooded me and I could barely breathe. As she went down the rows I paid no attention; all I could do was rehearse over and over what I would say. "My name is Nancy and my hobby is art." Sounds easy enough, but I managed to bungle those few simple words. Luckily, my voice was practically inaudible and no one heard me anyway.

Needless to say, junior high provided me with many awkward moments.

Ninth grade. A girl in Spanish class said, "You should meet Gary. He's cute and I think you'd like him." Me: "What would I say?" "Just be yourself and don't say anything." This comment still haunts me. Gary's and my paths never crossed.

Senior year. I was at my boyfriend's house with his family. His mom's neighbor was visiting and apparently noticed how quiet I was. Bob's mother said with a hint of scorn, "She's backward." Over the years I've been called "unsocialized" more than once.

My math teacher wrote in my yearbook, "Try to smile!"

Such are the travails of a shy nerd. People often mistake us for being arrogant, retarded, snobby, rude, or aloof, when all along we're just trying to fit in and think of something to say!

My First War

by Deborah Fruchey

My first war was Cowboys against Indians. I was less than five years old. Spaghetti Westerns on TV were the inspiration for all the kids on the block. Two things to know about Indians: they had the neatest costumes, and they always lost. Two things to know about Cowboys: they were our kind, and they won.

Drawn on strictly partisan lines, if you wanted to win, you had to be a cowboy. In backyard war, since the bullets were invisible, someone could hit you point blank, and you could still claim you were only wounded. Or sometimes, you could come back to life, and claim you'd only been pretending to be dead. Indians were sneaky like that, we thought. And of course, the ultimate trump card in backyard war, you could be killed over and over again with no ill effects. It was poor form to come back from the dead more than once in a single game.

Sooner or later, everybody got a turn to be a cowboy, and win, but being an Indian had its attractions. We knew that Indians could be useful and noble. Look at Tonto. The chance to wear feathers and fringe and paint, shoot arrows instead of bullets, and put up your palm and say "how" while looking dignified and stern, was often too tempting to resist.

My favorite gig was to be an Indian Princess. We did not know that the Chickasaw royal family was fictional, or anything about the many tribes. The Indian Princess had the prettiest long hair, the longest fringe, and was always fainting and being dragged off to safety and presumed marriage. Patriarchy was an equal opportunity employer for Indian females. I was just as likely to be carried off by a cowboy as a red-skinned brave. It was desirable to be dragged away by the enemy, who would be forced to lock you up but would love and long for you from afar and eventually, torn by his loyalties, would help you escape and then run away with you. Then the princess would make peace between her husband and her daddy, and all would be well until the next war, about 15 minutes from now.

The dynamics of these things still intrigue me, fifty years later, wise to the lies of history. How was it that female stereotypes trumped both cultures? What was a delicate Princess doing on the battlefield anyway? Why were we so sure that a noble enemy still deserved to lose? Was it only that "they" were not "us"? And is that not the basis of war from time immemorial?

The need to win was hard-wired so early. We did not mind dying so much. It didn't hurt, it didn't last, and involved lots of dramatic arm flinging and groans and convulsions. Actually being dead, however, meant you missed all the excitement. No more running around, no yelling, no clobbering anyone. And besides, someone had defeated you. Someone had been faster, better, stronger, had better aim. This was intolerable.

So, we switched sides every other time. Why play a game in which there can ONLY be winners and losers unless you get to win 50% of the time? And winning felt so good! Bottom line, winners were happy. Everybody loved them. Winners got everything.

Why is it we continue this into adulthood, when the odds of winning personally are so slight, when death is not temporary, and those who make it home are neither heroes nor happy? When a cranky government handout is the reward for being a Good Guy? And when is it now that we stop designating other races to be the Bad Guys, who can be killed no matter how beautiful or noble?

As for being a royal princess, an entire generation is through with that. What did fainting ever get us, except being dragged off by the enemy?

~~~~~~

Motherland

by Marilyn Tavlin

On August 29, 2005, while living in Los Angeles, I watched the news in horror as Hurricane Katrina bore down and took deadly aim at my hometown of New Orleans. Having left the City in 1994 to carve out a new life in California, New Orleans still tethered me tightly to her. This is my requiem for the City.

Long after the cameras have stopped rolling, and the artificial lights taken down, the darkness deepens. Long after the pomp and circumstance have come and gone, the only signs of life to be found are the spores of mold spreading their tentacles across the walls of the homes now laid to waste.

The lore was fed to the babies as soon as they could digest it. The big one. The one that would swallow the City. A city of gamblers riding their winning hands, double or nothing. Doubling for decades, and now, nothing.

The town now gone, nothing left, including my history. My baggage. My motherland.

The town where I spent my youth until I went bankrupt. Dragged kicking and screaming from the Oklahoma dustbowl of my birth. Away from my dead father, and the life he planned for us, to my mother's hometown, now mine.

A city of whores and blues and tawdry news, with enough booze to drown the town, New Orleans sits on top of herself—a parasitic twin—looking like a used-up, clown-painted Blanche du Bois, hefting up her heavy skirts and squatting, pissing on the City. A steady stream of smelly yellow that keeps the air wet, always wet. Standing guard over the City making sure no new thoughts get in and no closed minds leave.

Nothing to protect now. Houses strewn like spilled pieces of a Monopoly board, thrown in an angry huff by a losing child.

The scab of an old, festering wound ripped off, erupting with pus and blood, ugliness long buried now rising to the top. Where the dispossessed march miles across a bridge to higher ground, through dirty, brackish waters carrying children on their shoulders, only to be met with officers, guns drawn, bellowing, "Go back, we don't want you here!"

Where another bridge becomes the final resting place for more innocents trying to escape the flooded City on foot, shot dead by police for no other reason than being the wrong skin color in the wrong place.

Where the most educated and accomplished citizens spout rhetoric matching the belief systems of the most ignorant—separate and not equal.

Where poverty is a crime, and a surefire way to prison, or hell.

Only memories left now.

Dressing up for Sunday services and singing "Jesus Loves Me"—me, the daughter of a Jew—for the preacher, who gave my sister and me a nickel every time we sang.

Riding the small trains in City Park, where the canopy of live oaks held back the intense rays of sun, leaving the thick, wet air to melt pink cotton candy onto our hands and faces. The beautiful, proud horses on the carousel, carved to a heightened reality, painted with care and grace. The ones in the middle frozen in place...the outside and inner rows moving up and down around the circle, timed to the beat of the grand musical score.

Spending Sundays at Audubon Zoo, the old one, with the seal pond, and the animals in prisons, not "settings," looking back at us, reflecting our destiny.

Taking the streetcar down St. Claude Avenue to the meat market at St. Roch. Watching in horror as my mother picked out live chickens that were taken to the back and returned in a neat package, unmoving and headless, my sister and I fighting to hold the hand that did not contain the bag of murdered chickens.

A place with smells all its own. A walk down a Quarter street fills the nostrils with musty, dark, exotic, erotic scents. Turn a corner, and the sewers assault.

On summer evenings, magnolias, honeysuckle, and gardenias captivate with their sickly-sweet aromas. And the freshly mown lawns on the hottest days—the air so heavy and green with fragrance, you could taste it.

Our new home now is in a neighborhood of cookie-cutter houses, row upon row facing each other, inhabited by truly desperate housewives. Housewives like my mother. Her days spent in a roller-coaster haze of uppers and downers. A raven-haired, fiery Carmen in blood-red lipstick and wide, twirling circle skirts, exuding the only power she thought she had—that of the temptress.

The physical trappings were soon to become remnants of her former self, deeply buried with her dead husband's memory. Replaced with frumpy, oversized muumuus covering her widened body, her streaked gray hair pulled tightly back into an unkempt, long ponytail.

But, before the decline, there was a new husband to be found. Like George, my mother's married friend. The one who could have saved us. He took us on weekend drives to places down the road—quiet little towns filled with live oaks festooned with Spanish moss, from which he would fashion a necklace and tenderly place it over my head.

Other trips to bayous and waterways where little boats sat as far as the eye could see, their names painted in flowing script. And always, George found one with my name, and one with my sister's. Every single time. Too young to read then, I thought he was magical. We knew he loved us, but, in the end, he loved his wife more.

Then, Otis came into the picture, and all bets for salvation were off. Our descent into hell had begun, my mother's already well in motion. Running full steam ahead, up for days and nights on a diet pill buzz.

Combing her hair obsessively over a once-black velvet wrap, formerly signifying an evening of music and dinner, now a shroud, a dark witness to her inconsolability, a winter wonderland of dandruff snowflakes.

Her body folded into a heap over the Victrola playing the music from her former life, wailing with grief. Sometimes awakening the house to do her bidding on whatever project caught her manic fancy, like defrosting the freezer at 3:00 a.m. She, who would rather be caught dead than wash a dish.

Then the flip side—the downers, when she would lie in her darkened room for days, unconscious, leaving us to fend for ourselves, and to fend off Otis. The monster. He found himself in the perfect setting to discharge the considerable rage he had accumulated over a lifetime. Four little children given up to him to abuse as he chose, and he did, while serving us breakfasts of stale cornflakes and sour milk.

I made my mother smile once: I fell into one of the canals in our neighborhood, in the quicksand, sinking, terrorized, until my sister reached her hand out and saved me. Covered in slime, I walked for blocks down the street, the neighbor kids running ahead to tell my mother. And, seeing me, she smiled. Afterwards, she told the story often, always amused by my close call.

I tried many more times to make her smile—riding motorcycles and cars too fast, hitchhiking across a dangerous town, hooking up with little and big criminals, carving my arms with razor-bladed vitriol—on and on, yet never did she smile at me again.

She, so like my city. My hometown. My motherland. The two interwoven into one symbiotic identity that formed and shaped me.

New Orleans seduced me with her siren call, and wove her web tightly around me, locking me firmly in place like the tentacles of mold on the walls of the homes now laid to waste.

~~~~~~~

Becoming Godparents in the Land of the Mayas

by Merrilee Cavenecia

Pine Mountain

Some years ago, my husband, Frank, and I decided to travel to the very southern part of Mexico—to the state of Chiapas, following the Maya trail, starting at the town of San Cristobal de las Casas and moving on to Palenque. We never dreamed of becoming godparents to a Lacandon Maya baby!

Dusk fell on that July day as we entered the cab at the airport in Tuxtla Gutierrez. We began a three-hour ride up the mountain to reach our first destination, San Cristobal de las Casas, a small town in the highlands of southern Mexico, the heart of Maya country.

We quickly passed through the outskirts of Tuxtla and began our ascent on the two-lane highway. Small houses built of mud brick or cinder block and covered with gray corrugated tin roofs appeared sporadically on the sides of the road, often not just homes to families, but also small grocery stores or restaurants with a few tables and folding chairs, serving corn roasted over outdoor barbecues, fresh tortillas, black bean tacos, and tamales. Others were stores with displays of local artisans—white blouses with colorful embroidered designs, woven belts, ethnic pottery, and the ever-present tourist T-shirts.

Within a short time, we no longer saw people on the roadsides; the houses became farther and farther apart. The road continued to climb, and the last traces of daylight forced our eyes to exert themselves in order to see the unfamiliar shapes of trees, shrubs, and small houses at the sides of the road.

As I squinted my eyes in that grayness that separated day and night, inside of me was a sense of a secret being revealed. On this special road, I felt a beauty emanating out of the very soul of the earth, a beauty that touched me even when only that enveloping grayness was visible. Something mysterious.

The road continued to climb and as it did it narrowed. We hugged the edges of the mountain—around and back around we went—the road a thin gray ribbon, in the gray of that in-between time. Perhaps some deity had granted man permission to drape this road onto the mountain.

The taxi traversed the road at a speed only possible by a driver who can anticipate each curve, his knowledge emerging from memories thoroughly embedded in the folds of the brain, a near unconscious knowing of how each cut of the road is woven into the mountain. At such speed, and with grayness turning to blackness, mere shadows of trees and shrubs were obliterated. We looked into the accelerated blackness while our bodies swung back and forth with the increasing and sharpening curves. A familiar aroma crept through the cracks of the windows. It permeated the air. We were traveling through a pine forest.

Now it was totally black outside. Our eyes searched for something on which to focus. Tiny spots of light appeared randomly, dotting the hillsides. No pattern could be found. The lights of newly acquired electricity sparkled on the mountain—one home, one wire, one light bulb—each home tucked into its particular fold of this pine mountain.

We turned another curve and the road and surrounding hills were suddenly flooded with a silvery light. A full moon, so large it made us gasp, sat at the top of a mountain peak, raining moonlight on all below, as though no separation existed between the mountaintop and the moon with no sky in between. The moon had come down from its distant home to visit us. We gaped, trying to swallow it with our eyes. As quickly as it appeared, it disappeared with the next curve of the road. Like children, we peered out every window, yearning to see it again. Then, it smiled down on us again, touching the top of the hill, like a gigantic silver jewel, and disappeared. It became a game. From which direction would she reveal herself next—this laughing, shining medallion in the sky that kept peeking down at us from one mountaintop and then another, seeming to roll playfully across the tips of the pine trees.

We were not the only ones enthralled by this moon lady who visits both the pine-covered highlands and the rainforest lowlands of southern Mexico. In ancient Mayan times, she was Akena, "Our Mother." As she traveled across the night sky, she became weaker until at daybreak she descended to the underworld, where she was cared for by Sukunkyum, the first Mayan god to be born from the *bak nikte* flower. Fed and carried through the underworld, she was resurrected, strong and rested, at the next moonrise. No doubt she was full of energy on this night as she bounced from mountaintop to mountaintop.

When it seemed that the climb up the mountain would continue on endlessly, we started to descend. Within a few minutes, the lights of a small city emerged below us. It was San Cristobal. Just as suddenly, we were in this valley city, on ancient cobblestone streets that held the width of one car and were bounded by eighteen-inch high curbs—so that in the rainy season there would be plenty of room for the water that rushed down the mountains to be channeled into the narrow streets so as not to enter any buildings. Houses were hidden behind tall concrete walls and iron gates, separating public sidewalk and private property. As it was now evening, storeowners had pulled the corrugated gray metal doors down over the fronts of their shops. All was dark except the headlights of the taxi, the occasional lights of a café still open for business, and the moon lady, now high above us—having withdrawn from her roly-poly game of hide and seek in the folds of the pine mountain, she sedately lit our way.

Our destination was Na Bolom—a museum, a retreat for artists, and an inn, where we would be guests.

We stopped in front of a block-long, six-foot-high stone wall, which contained one heavy, wooden double door. We rang the bell while the taxi driver plopped our suitcases onto the cobblestone sidewalk. We looked at each other—hoping that there would be an answer. Then the door opened. A young American woman with short black hair, jeans, and a red T-shirt said they had been waiting for us.

We were now in a courtyard with trees and flowering plants in profusion.

"Your room is at the top of the hill," she said.

Passing through another heavy wooden door, we entered a garden that led to a pathway full of pebbles and unevenly laid stones, marked at the edges by glass bottles turned upside down and dug into the earth. Trees, bushes, and flowers extended on both sides of the curving path—into the night. We continued up the hill, the black-haired girl well ahead of us, as her familiarity with the path hastened her steps. Our friend, the moon, poked fingers of light onto the path for us.

We arrived at a little bungalow at the top of the hill and stepped into a small room with a big fireplace of gray stone. On the mantle stood several clay pots about six inches in diameter. At the front of each, a face was pinched onto the rim and painted in red and black, a Lacandon Maya incense burner, called a god pot. This was our first welcome by the Lacandon Mayas.

I turned a god pot around in my fingers, touching antiquity gingerly. I had read that the Lacandon people were allowed to stay at Na Bolom without charge. *Perhaps I will see some of these people*, I thought.

In our room, the red tile floor was covered with a number of animal skins. I lightly fingered the short dark brown hair of one of the skins. Maybe it's a goat, I thought, or the skin of some jungle creature that I don't know.

The small double bed was covered with at least seven hand-woven blankets, some of cotton, others of wool, each with different geometric designs in all arrays of colors—blacks, reds, yellows, whites, greens, blues—blankets from the indigenous artisans of San Cristobal.

We lit the fire in the huge fireplace, sat down on chairs draped with Indian blankets, wriggled our toes on animal-skin rugs and inhaled the combined smell of moist must from thick adobe walls and bone-dry pine burning voraciously in the fireplace while the Lacandon Maya god pots sat silently on the mantle, observing.

The Dining Room

One-thirty, time of the mid-day meal. We joined the other guests gathering in the dining room of Na Bolom. It held one very long rectangular table that seated twenty people.

The artwork of past artists in residence, as well as photographs taken by Trudy Blom, covered three walls. She and her archaeologist husband, Franz Blom, founded this combination of museum, artist's retreat, and inn more than a half-century ago. Trudy, now ninety years old, was still a recognized photographer. Her work spanned a fifty-year period, creating a photographic history of the life and people of Chiapas. Some knew her as the "queen of the rainforest."

Particularly striking was the framed photograph on one wall of a Lacandon Maya man. With flowing black hair parted down the middle and wearing a long-sleeved, knee-length white gown, he stood before the backdrop of the jungle.

Trudy then entered the dining room, holding a black-lacquered cane in her right hand. Short white hair, carefully waved and combed, framed her face. Her make-up and lipstick were perfectly done. Dressed in a floor-length turquoise dress with long flowing sleeves, a printed silk scarf draped her shoulders. Strands of colorful beads and a chained silver medallion hung around her neck. On both wrists, she wore wide silver bracelets. Her fingers were bedecked with silver rings holding large stones set in bold swirls of intricately worked designs. She walked slowly, imperiously, to her seat at the head of the table.

She came to San Cristobal as a woman in her forties, a Swiss socialist journalist, and a trained horticulturalist, having suffered the devastation of World War II. She came to Mexico with her camera and, perhaps, with her hopes. She met Franz Blom and they started a life together. Na Bolom, at the time they purchased it, was an old and run-down house, built in the Spanish style around a courtyard. They gradually restored it and made it their home.

As she traveled with her husband to uncover Mayan archaeological sites, she took pictures of the people who lived in the area—men, women and children, dressed in long white tunics, living in houses covered with thatch and with walls made of slender poles. She met these Lacandon Maya people, who slept in woven hammocks, cooked over outdoor fires, and bathed themselves in the nearby river.

She saw how they planted their *milpas*, their fields, with corn and beans and chilies, with papayas and bananas and avocadoes. She watched them raise their chickens and hunt with hand-carved bows and arrows in the jungle. She and Franz became good friends with them.

They not only became good friends, but they devoted their lives toward preserving the Lacantún rainforest, the home of the Lacandon. They also showed their lifelong commitment to these people by keeping rooms available for them at Na Bolom. The rooms were always free of charge, as were the daily meals. It allowed the Lacandons to come to the city to sell their handicrafts, such as necklaces made of bone and seed, and handmade bows and arrows. This was Franz and Trudy's gift to their friends who lived in the Lacantún forest.

~~~~~

One Mayan family sitting at the far end of the table included a young man and woman with a baby, and an older woman. They watched Trudy without seeming to, knowing that she would soon get up to leave the table, the signal that they had permission to leave also. They ate quietly, without speaking, most of the time with their eyes down, not venturing into conversations with the other guests.

The young man, who, we found out later, was named Ishmael, had pitch-black hair, cut short in Western style, cut before coming into town so that he would fit in with the townspeople and not be stared at. At home in his village, he let it grow again, down to his shoulders, parting it in the middle, as was the Lacandon custom. The jeans and T-shirt he wore were comfortable enough, although he missed the freedom of the white tunic that he wore at home. Nevertheless, he was accustomed to switching into these clothes when he came into San Cristobal to sell his

~~~~~

Trudy rose to leave the table. We and the other guests also began to leave.

As we walked out onto the patio, we saw that Ishmael and his family were sitting together outside on a bench. My husband went up to them.

"May I take your picture?" he asked in Spanish, smiling, shaking hands as is the custom and then inviting them to our room. The conversation and friendship began.

We asked Ishmael what his Mayan name was.

"Well, my Spanish name is Ishmael," he said. "That's the name they gave me when I went to school in San Cristobal. I went to school at first with my long hair but I had to cut it and I had to wear Western clothes. I only stayed in school for two years, just to learn to read and write, but then I abandoned it. But the name I really like is my Mayan name—Chan Sap Yuk."

"Will you write it down for us?" my husband asked.

Ishmael took the notebook and pen that we handed to him. Carefully he wrote his name in strong bold print, translating the meaning of each word into Spanish. Chan meaning small, Sap meaning a star, and Yuk meaning a deer, a small deer-shaped star. Could it mean that his name came from the generations of Mayans who peered at the night skies of the rainforest and saw a small deer in the starry heavens?

Ishmael's wife, Chanuc, sat across from us, holding the baby, a little girl four-and-a-half months old. Wearing a red and pink V-neck dress and Pampers, her round moon face was framed by short black hair. She looked out at the world through big dark eyes, and her smiles were so spontaneous they warmed our hearts. Chanuc, her long black hair reaching well below her shoulders, held her daughter in a cloth carrier so the baby was snuggling in front of her. Even when the baby wiggled just a little, Chanuc immediately nursed her.

After we talked for a while, I stood and walked over to her to get a closer look at the baby, and Chanuc held the baby out, inviting me to hold her. I spoke to her in a mixture of Spanish and English. The way she reached out her little hands and made that infectious baby gurgle, smiling so joyfully, filled me with such love.

I looked at Chanuc, "Thank you for letting me hold her," I said. "She's so beautiful!"

As I rocked the baby, we continued talking. We asked how she met her husband, and this was when Chanuc began giggling.

"Oh, he was supposed to marry someone else. He was even going to start supporting her by doing things like buying oil for cooking for her. That's what a man does to show he is going to marry a girl. Then, I saw him in my father's store. I smiled and laughed. If a girl does that, it means that she loves him. I also went to his house and told him the other girl didn't really love him but that I did. And so we married!" Chanuc laughed—looking at Ishmael.

"I didn't want to be like my sister. She's married to a seventy-year-old man. I didn't want that to happen to me!" She giggled and looked again at Ishmael.

As we sat there in our room, both Chanuc and Ishmael observed everything so carefully, noticing the god pots on the fireplace mantle.

"Can you tell us about these?" I asked.

"Oh yes, they are part of our Mayan religion," Ishmael answered. "They are some of our gods. The Christian missionaries didn't want us to use them, but Chanuc and I decided, when we married, we would follow the old religion, to keep the traditions. That's what we want to do."

We also noticed they were looking at the tile floor, so I decided to ask about their house.

Ishmael said, "We have a dirt floor and a thatched roof. We could get corrugated tin roofs but they make the house too hot and also they are too noisy when it rains. The rain has a quiet sound on the thatch."

"And do you have electricity?" my husband asked.

"We have one light bulb. We just got it last May. We'd really like to put a light over our cooking area but we need a piece of cord to connect it. That's expensive."

Frank and I looked at each other.

"Maybe we can help you get that," Frank said.

They looked at each other. Chanuc smiled. Ishmael rubbed his head, looked down, nodded, deep in thought. As the time was getting late and we wanted to talk more, we decided to invite them for lunch the next day at a local café where we had plans to eat. We agreed to meet there at noon. Then they surprised us.

Baptism at Palenque

"Yes," we had said. "We will be baby Chanakin's godparents. We will give her a baptismal name and be connected with her for a lifetime."

We all agreed that this would be a Mayan ceremony, and what place could be better than at the great pyramids of Palenque, the Mayan ancestral home.

Two days later, we drove down the windy, mountain road from San Cristobal to Palenque. The pyramids stretched into the sky from their bed in the jungle, a jungle that had hidden them for centuries, centuries since their glory in 700 A.D., yet now rediscovered, unearthed, deeply studied—some of the most masterful and meaningful of all Mexican pyramids. And that would be where this little Lacandon Maya baby would be baptized in the glory of her ancestors' past.

The four of us and baby Chanakin met at Palenque in the early morning, before the heat of the midday. For the ceremony, Ishmael and Chanuc asked us to bring some corn tortillas as well as a bottle of purified water, these being symbolic of the main ingredients for life, and used as part of the baptism. We asked no questions, for they would guide us in how to perform this Lacandon Maya tradition.

As we lined up to pay the entrance fee, Ishmael was shocked. "Are they going to charge a Mayan person to see his own ancestral home?" We had no answer.

On first seeing the immense pyramid called the Temple of Inscriptions, Chanuc's mouth fell open, her eyes grew huge as she took in its magnificence. She peered up silently, staring at the multiple layers of stairs leading to a large building at the top, with five wide doorways serving as entrances. Both Chanuc and Ishmael stood transfixed.

"Our ancestors built this," Ishmael whispered to Chanuc. "Let's go up," Chanuc said. Ishmael nodded.

We intervened at this point.

"Why don't we do the baptism first and then explore?" suggested my husband. "You'll need to decide on where you want to do it." They agreed.

We continued walking, coming to the Palace complex, a group

of several connected buildings as well as courtyards and terraces. Ishmael and Chanuc kept staring at the trees behind some of the structures. We watched and followed, realizing they were thinking of a jungle setting, away from pathways and buildings.

"Let's go in this direction," she said as she pointed toward a place behind the Palace. We walked across a small bridge that took us to the edge of the jungle.

"Here," she pointed at a stone bench between two small trees, a bench made from a stone from one of the pyramids.

We gathered around the bench, taking out the tortillas and purified water from our backpack.

"Now we will lay Chanakin on the bench," she said. The bench became a resting place for the baby as she gently laid her upon it. Chanakin's red-and-pink print dress draped around her round four-month-old body and her fluffy short black hair framed her moon-shaped face. She contentedly looked up at her mama.

"And now," Chanuc said to me, "you will pick her up and hold her on your left hip."

I carefully picked her up. We seemed to already know each other, for she made a little gurgling sound and settled herself comfortably. Chanuc smiled, brushing her long black hair back from her face, and then stepped back. The ceremony began.

While we would all stay together, Ishmael took the lead, giving me directions about what I should say to Chanakin during each part of the ceremony.

He led us into the adjacent jungle where trees glistened in many shades of green.

"This will be your home," I told her. "This is where you will live."

We walked amongst the trees, feeling the warm air and breathing in the moisture emanating from the soil and tropical trees, and stopped at a wild banana tree.

"From banana trees like this and other fruit trees in our jungle, you will gather food to eat," I told her. As we stood there, with the huge leaves and bananas decorating the branches, Chanakin stretched out a chubby hand. Was she reaching for a banana? I didn't know but I smiled down at her. She seemed cozily comfortable sitting on my left hip.

Ishmael had brought the bottle of purified water with him and now he held it out. He had me cup my hand so he could pour some water into it. I put some of the water into Chanakin's hands and on her head.

"This is the water you will use to wash with, so that you will be clean," I told her.

Chanakin wiggled her fingers together, feeling the water slide on her skin. When I put some water on her head, she giggled, seeming to enjoy feeling her hair get a little wet.

Then Ishmael had me cup my hands again and let Chanakin lean over and taste the cool water as I told her, "This is also the water you will drink when you are thirsty."

She licked her lips, the cool water so refreshing in the moist heat.

We continued to walk deeper into the woods, hearing the sounds of the forest, birds calling to each other and the rustle of leafy trees as the tropical breeze whispered through their branches. We stopped not far from a large tree and Ishmael explained what I should tell Chanakin.

"This is where you'll do your 'poo poo,'" I said, "far away from the house, out here in the forest."

He had me hold her down in a squatting position, her little bare feet touching the moist earth, the ground lightly covered with dry fallen leaves as well as sprouts of new growth. She looked at me and listened, letting her toes wiggle across the soft earth.

It was time to leave the forest setting and return once again to the stone bench. Asking us to take out the tortillas, I held out a tortilla to Chanakin and she grasped it with one chubby little hand, holding it tightly. She didn't want to let it go.

"This is what you'll learn to cook, just like your mother does," I told her. "You'll learn to grind the corn and you'll make wonderful tortillas for all of your family."

After giving her time to hold the tortilla, I was to lay her once again upon the bench, while we carefully removed the tortilla from her hand and set it down at the end of the bench.

I stepped back. Now was the time for Frank to pick her up. Placing her on his left hip as I had done, we again entered the forest.

When it was time for her to be introduced to water, she was eager to sip it as Frank cupped his hand and explained that this is what she would drink when she was thirsty. Frank watched intently as Chanakin leaned forward to sip the water from his cupped hand. He so carefully placed his hand in just the right position so it would be easy for Chanakin to take a little sip.

Just as I had explained to Chanakin, so also did Frank: water was to wash; the surrounding forest her home, a place where she would find sustenance from the bounty of the jungle.

After stopping at the wild banana tree, Ishmael led Frank and Chanakin to another tree, similar to a palm tree, explaining that this tree gave food both from its leaves when they were cooked but also from its branches which, when cracked open, offered additional food.

"These are the trees you will use to provide food for your family," Frank told her. "These and so many others which grow in this jungle where you will live and raise your family."

Chanakin reached out toward the tree, then nuzzled her head against Frank's shoulder.

We all returned to the stone bench and Frank gently laid her upon it.

Now, was the time to give Chanakin her baptismal name. We had chosen the name "Esperanza," which means hope in Spanish, a name that represented a future of opportunity for this little baby girl, this little Lacandon Maya girl who we had been given the chance to meet.

"We'd like to give her the name, 'Esperanza,'" Frank said, "for she represents hope for the new generation of Lacandon Mayas."

Chanuc's face lit up, her smile showed it all.

"Yes," Ishmael said, "Yes—Chanakin Esperanza, a name that will represent the best for her as she grows into the future."

"Now, we will seal our *'compadrismo,'*" Ishmael said, "by sharing tortillas together."

We were all full of smiles. Joy filled the air as we enjoyed nibbling the sweet corn tortillas. Even Chanakin had a chance once again to hold tightly to a tortilla.

We prepared to leave the baptismal site, gathering our belongings, for it was time to explore.

Chanuc led the way with baby Chanakin Esperanza held safely on her hip. We walked back again toward the Palace complex. With Chanuc in the lead, up they went, up the many steep stairs and into the tower. We watched from below. What they climbed in a few minutes would have taken us so much longer, even if we had the nerve to ascend those high steep steps with no banisters and only one rope in the middle to steady oneself. Slightly out of breath, but with smiles on their faces, they joined us again after their climb.

We walked on to the Temple of Inscriptions, the tallest pyramid at Palenque. The inscriptions inside the temple tell the history of the city and its most famous leader, Pakal. That is where Ishmael and Chanuc headed next. With Chanakin on her hip, they ascended the pyramid, waving to us from the top.

Soon it was time to leave. Ishmael and Chanuc would return to their village, Lacanja, still another seven hours of travel into the heart of the jungle. We would return to the States. We agreed to stay in touch with each other through Na Bolom, for they stayed there whenever they went into San Cristobal, and we would call as well.

When it was time to say goodbye, I had tears in my eyes. How could I have imagined when we first drove up the pine mountain to San Cristobal, or even when we learned of Trudi Blom's connections to the Lacandon Mayas, that we would become godparents to a Lacandon Maya baby? An adventure on the Maya trail had become a life-altering event, as I was Chanakin's godmother and our worlds would forever be connected.

Visions

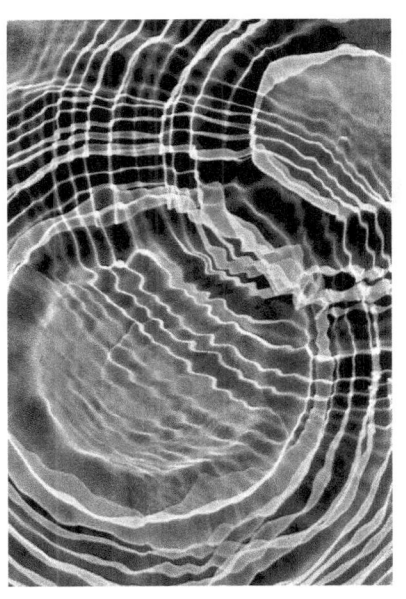

~~~~~

Mars in Opposition

by Rob Rogers

I ease into the chair across from the console and stare at the frozen image of what used to be my face. The transmission is out of joint, but that should change soon. Mars and Earth are in opposition. This is as clear as things are likely to get for a long time.

He's thinner than he was when I last saw him. Paler, too, though not jaundiced—none of the symptoms I've been taught to look for. And he's disappointed.

"She's not coming?" he asks. The words arrive a few seconds after he says them, something that would be disorienting coming from anyone else. But we've never had any problems understanding each other. It's one of the reasons NASA continues to arrange these conversations.

"Not this time."

"She heard," he says, which is, as he knows, something of an understatement. My wife, whom he had expected to see, and on whose behalf he has probably spent the better part of a day rehearsing an apology, found out about the affair at the same time the rest of the world did, when photos from what was supposed to be a restricted feed surfaced online last night. Privacy is one of the first things you lose, being an astronaut.

Not that I would know.

"She knew it would happen," I tell him. "She just didn't think it would be this soon."

He nods, distracted, and I realize he has something important to tell me. I wonder, for a moment, if he is going to tell me about her. Dr. Wiest. Katherine. Tall and thin, with high cheekbones—"a Q-Tip," my wife had snorted, when she heard the news. I had never thought of the Earthbound version of Dr. Wiest as anything more than an astrobiologist. But things on Mars, as I am sure he is about to tell me yet again, always turn out differently than we expect.

He still uses the "we" when talking about us—he and I—even though we are no longer the same person, have not been since the I that we were stepped onto the telepad in Houston two years ago.

They say that it is impossible to remember. What they really mean is that no one who has gone through the process of quantum teleportation has, as yet, found the words to describe the experience. In one moment I am Schrodinger's cat, there and here at the same time, a soul undivided across hundreds of thousands of miles of radiation and emptiness. I am simultaneously the man who has dreamed and studied and built and trained his entire life to stand on the surface of another planet and the one who is already there. Then he steps forward, and I step back, and for that moment and always we become he, and I.

Which is an easier concept to understand than it was to explain to my parents.

"He's not a copy of me. That is, he won't be," I told them, months before the event in question became a matter of public record. "Neither of us will be a copy of the other."

My mother tried to be helpful. "It's like when you cut a worm in half," she shouted into my father's good ear. "Each half grows back into its own version of the original."

"Sounds painful," my father said. "Why don't they just send you in the rocket?"

My mother sighed, exasperated. "They don't send people up in rockets any more. Only robots," she said. "The robots build the— what do you call it? Not a house—the habitat. They set everything going, build the telepad. Then the astronauts can just walk in like they're walking through a door."

"So you'll never get to see the planet from space," my father said. "Either of them."

"But that doesn't matter. He'll be on Mars!" my mother said.

My father turned to look at me, then, with an expression I couldn't read, or didn't want to. "And Diana is okay with this?"

"She won't even have to miss him," my mother said, her voice a little louder than it really needed to be. "He'll be here on Earth, too, right here for her."

"Not all of him will," my father said. At the time, it hadn't seemed like a big deal.

The part of me that made it to Mars says, "They're going to ask you to fix the robots. Don't. There's nothing wrong with them."

Time and words are precious, doubly so when speaking across worlds. We have never been ones for small talk. In the past, it has always been a relief not to have to ask how he is feeling, or what he's been thinking about. He is not going to tell me how it feels to hold Katherine Wiest any more than I would consider telling him what it felt like to make love last week to my wife, a woman he is unlikely to come within a hundred thousand miles of throughout the rest of his life.

The transition still feels abrupt.

"What's wrong with them…the robots?"

We both understand that we are not talking about the station AI, or the clumsy but reliable rovers that roll around the planet's surface, taking a beating so that we…so that people like him… don't have to, or the orbiters, which rely on the same quantum technology that separated us to relay our words across oceans of soundless space. We are talking about the swarms of anthropods for which he and I are directly responsible. Our life's work. The reason we were chosen for this mission.

There was a time when neither of us would have referred to the 'pods as "robots," when my wife had to warn me not to get defensive whenever anyone failed to grasp right away what it was that made them so special.

"They're bureaucrats, honey," my wife said on the morning of the demonstration. "You're going to have to explain things to them two or three times before they get it."

"But this is NASA," I said. "Computer scientists. Engineers. How is distributed artificial intelligence any harder to understand than quantum computing?"

"They'll never let you talk to the engineers, dear," my wife said in that tone of voice that tells me when I am on the verge of becoming unreasonable. "The people you'll be talking to are the ones whose job it is to keep everyone else at NASA from spending money. That means they're going to ask a lot of stupid questions, and you're going to have to act as though they're brilliant and insightful."

I must have made a face, because she said, "You spent five years teaching a cockroach to navigate a maze. You can take two hours to teach a roomful of admirals and politicians why the space program needs your astropods."

I kept that in mind—not her words so much as the smooth, calming melody of her voice—as the people who would decide whether I was indispensable enough to send to Mars poked and prodded at the workers humming and flying and building around them and asked their stupid questions.

"So the queen tells the other robots what to do?"

"There is no queen," I told them, remembering to maintain eye contact. "Each anthropod performs several specific functions and transmits details about everything it encounters to the other members of the swarm, which collectively processes the information and incorporates it into the development of the next generation."

"Can you give us an example?" asked a woman in a white dress uniform, staring at me through glasses with thin, copper-colored frames.

"Of course," I said. "These anthropods over here—the, uh, blue ones—have discovered that the mixture of gases in this room runs too high to nitrogen. They're releasing a chemical that tells workers on the other side of the colony to plant more nitrogen-fixing crops."

"Like beans," the uniformed woman said.

"Sure. And then these, uh, green ones—the builders—they've learned that the surface of this table is much smoother than expected. They're kind of slipping and sliding all over the place. Assuming that I let this demonstration run for the next 48 hours, the next generation of workers would probably have something on their feet that made it easier to grip the surface. Little claws, maybe. Or skid pads. Or suction cups, though that's unlikely."

"Don't you know?" the woman asked.

I shook my head. "Previous exploration campaigns have depended on the somewhat arrogant assumption that we could prepare our technology for anything it might encounter. That's why Mars is littered with broken robots. The anthropod swarm evaluates each situation without prejudice, on a moment-to-moment basis, and adapts itself accordingly, thus freeing it from the limits of human imagination."

The woman in uniform had said nothing then. A few days after the demonstration, I received a handwritten note. "You have created something capable of living in the moment while putting the needs of the next generation above its own. That is an achievement," she wrote. Had she been there when I received it, I might have pointed out to her that every living thing on Earth does exactly that, and always has, except for us.

Then again, I might not have. None of us really knows what we would do in a given situation until we are there.

"The robots," I say, choosing my words very carefully, "are adapting to their environment in ways we did not anticipate."

It is a statement, not a question. There are only two reasons why he might have referred to the anthropods as "robots." The first has to do with vocabulary. NASA has promised both of us that these infrequent conversations will remain private and encrypted. In practice that means any utterance of a particular keyword—"life support," or "critical," or any of several dozen others that we know about—will cause their algorithm to flag this segment of the transmission for review. "Anthropod" is one of those words.

The other reason is that he knows I have the ability, and the responsibility, to shut down the anthropod swarm remotely if circumstances call for it. It's one of the only really useful functions NASA has assigned to me and not him, though both of us assumed I'd never have to exercise it.

"Unexpected, but better," he insists. "New designation of workers. New hierarchies. The generational cycle has shifted to reflect the rhythm of the Martian day. We think they may be using new chemical compounds to communicate."

"You don't know?" I ask, reminding myself of the woman with copper-rimmed eyes.

He approaches his words with equal deliberation. "The activities of some of the…robots…have placed them in situations where observation has become difficult."

The scientist in me—the version of myself I see, fully realized, on the screen in front of me—wants to ask for details about these transformations, wants to know how the children of my mind have collectively overcome the challenges of an alien landscape and become alien themselves. It is, however, the washout—the homebody, the one left behind—who locks onto the eyes of his other self and asks, "Are they posing any danger to the crew? Or the mission?"

"Quite the opposite," he says, too quickly, as if he had been anticipating my question, which of course he had. "Ka…Dr. Wiest was just remarking this morning that it's becoming easier to breathe in the habitat."

I let myself imagine the circumstances under which that conversation took place: over a cup of tea in the commissary? Kneeling, side by side, in the garden? Or slowly disentangling from an embrace, his hand leaving little wakes in a crimson river of unspooled hair? And where could they have gone? The habitat was never built for privacy, or for passion. Until recently, I would have said the same thing about him and me.

"They've found a way to increase the oxygen content."

"No," he says, waiting for me to figure it out, a habit my wife has always found annoying. I resolve to let her know she is right, as usual.

"Your bodies are adapting to the atmosphere?"

"I wouldn't have noticed if Dr. Wiest hadn't said the coffee tasted different," he says. "They've been putting…something in our food and drink that makes it easier for our bodies to handle the extra nitrogen."

"They're not supposed to have access to the food supply."

He stares back at me without saying anything. We both knew it was only a matter of time before the anthropods found their way into every aspect of the ecosystem.

"It will show up in the crew logs, if it hasn't already," he says. "We're all sleeping better. Breathing easier. Adjusting faster than anyone had predicted to the longer days, the drop in gravity."

"You're becoming Martians."

"Yes," he says, and there is pride in his voice.

"That's going to be a problem once the next crew comes in."

"Maybe," he says. "The next crew won't notice that much of a difference. The one after that…" His eyes lose their focus for a moment, then return to me. "It's possible that the robots will have modified the teleporter to the extent that the next crew will arrive with a Martian physiology, and never know the difference."

"That's not possible," I say, a little louder than I had intended. "Teleportation is a quantum event. Whatever is in one place is exactly the same as what appears in the other."

I don't say, *We were the same person, once.* I shouldn't have to.

"Yes and no," he says. "Isn't that what teleportation is? A window opens, and what was possible before becomes actual; what had been actual becomes one of many possibilities. I remember my wedding day. Fishing with Grandpa. The taste of barbecued tri-tip fresh from the smoker. But these feet have never walked on grass. Flowing water has never touched these hands. I will never know what it is to walk in the open air. But my grandchildren will. They will grow up under orange skies, dancing and dreaming by the light of two moons, and they will look at this place"—he gestures around the habitat—"as a nursery, as the greenhouse where life from the mother planet first took root in a new world."

For the first time in all of our conversations, I feel the weight of the distance between us.

"You and Dr. Wiest have talked about children?" The Katherine Wiest I know is tall, angular, and severe, as focused on her sugar beets and hydroponic tubes of blue-green algae as I am...as I was...on the anthropods. I can no more imagine her as a mother than I could envision a parking lot in bloom.

"We live close to the edge of death," he says, nodding to the several centimeters-thick aluminum and steel habitat walls that to him, I'm sure, feel no more secure than a canvas tent in a monsoon. "I suppose that has made us consider the possibilities of life."

"What you're considering," I say, "is changing, fundamentally, what it means to be human."

"And what exactly do you mean by 'human'?" he asks. "The primate mind that assumes itself to be in charge? Or the thousands of other organisms—the bacteria, the mites—that live on us and in us, that exert their influence in ways that seem imperceptible, but nevertheless shape who we become?"

He pauses, and for a moment seems actually to be embarrassed. "I know you'll say that's Katherine talking."

"No," I say. "I think it's the swarm talking. We wanted so badly to live on another world that we built something smart enough to help us survive. We just forgot to tell it not to change who we are in the process of doing so. That's a mistake I won't make the second time around."

In the time it takes for our transmissions to pass in the ether I ask myself why he has chosen to tell me all of this. My motives for doing things were never altogether clear to me when I was only one person, and I have never been good at reading the hidden agendas of others.

When he finally speaks, he is quoting Thoreau.

"'Things do not change; we change,'" he says. "We have to. If humanity wants to extend its reach to the stars it can't go wandering through the cosmos like a tourist, hoping to leave its mark on every other world it passes without being changed in the process."

"The only reason anyone outside of Houston still supports the idea of space exploration is that they . . ." I pause, and correct myself. "Is that *we* want to look up in the sky and believe it could be us up there. Or our children. When they learn that nothing and no one can hope to survive outside the Earth without becoming fundamentally different from what they were..."

He interrupts, which given the time it takes our words to reach each other means that he cannot possibly have heard the last several things I said, which means he already knew what I was going to say.

"The only people who will notice are those who have too much invested in the project to want to do anything about it," he says. "And you. And you know better. You told them—we told them— the reason why every other mission to Mars failed was that we tried to act like farmers. Like gardeners. When really we're just one of the crops in the garden. We have to have the humility to see ourselves as part of a system."

"That we *built*," I say, my fingers drifting toward the keyboard. The shutdown code—a sequence of numbers and letters that will strip the life force from our Pinocchio—lies on a little notepad next to the screen. "Where is the humility in that? Maybe you can't say it. Maybe they've changed you so much that you can't even see it. But you know what we have to do."

I brace myself in anticipation of his anger. I expect him to shout, to slam his fist, to curse me and NASA and storm out of the room, chair spinning, the violence of his outburst serving as a kind of consolation for the immensity of his loss. It is, after all, what I would do in his situation.

Instead he sits back, sighs, and stares directly at me—not at the camera, or my face on the screen, but at me. "I'm sorry," he says.

"We always knew there could be problems with the..."

"I'm sorry that I'm here, and you're there," he says, putting into words what neither of us has ever acknowledged. "To believe your entire life that you're meant to do one thing—to put everything you have toward that goal—and then not only to have it snatched away from you, but to have to watch while someone else seems to be squandering what you wanted, is a terrible thing."

I realize I am holding my breath, and let it go.

"The way you talk about it, you'd think you were the one going through it," I tell him.

"It's what I planned to say to Diana," he says.

I waste valuable seconds processing what he has said.

"You think I'm squandering my relationship with her?" I ask.

"I think the same thing you probably think of me," he says. "That you're doing the best you can, under the circumstances. But that I'd do a better job than you, if only I had the opportunity to do so."

My eyes drift toward the notepad and its numbers. "So you're asking for the benefit of the doubt," I said. "That, having identified a possible defect in the system, I should allow it to continue because your possibly compromised instincts tell you it's the right thing to do."

"Do you remember the last time we trusted our instincts?" he says.

"I'm sorry," I say, picking up the notebook. "I really am. But..."

"California," he says. It's all he has to say.

It's the story our father told at our wedding, how the first and only time his son disappointed him was when he dropped out of graduate school, abandoned a scholarship, ignored the good advice of his family and all his friends, and drove for two days straight from Houston to Berkeley, all to follow a girl who never seemed all that interested in him to begin with.

"And that," our father said, raising his glass to cheers and smiles and the embarrassed blushing of Diana and me, "turned out to be the best decision he ever made."

"Diana still thinks we were crazy to do it," I say.

"She thought it was out of character," he says. "Which it was. She thought we'd hate it in California. That we'd miss our job and our family and that we'd blame her for everything we gave up to be with her."

"We…kind of did," I say.

"Change doesn't happen overnight," he says, his voice low and steady, like hers. "But it's possible, when the motivation is strong enough. Even for us."

"Is that what you want me to tell her?" I say. I pick up the notebook, then flip to the next sheet in the pad. I reach for the jar of pens next to the keyboard.

"Tell her I'm sorry. No," he says. "Tell her I would give anything just to be in the room with her, breathing the air of her resentment. To feel her hand slapping my face would be an incalculable gift."

"I don't know that she'll understand," I say, though we both know that I am wrong.

~~~~~

Party Time

by Becky Bishop White

"When your number's up, it's up," Robert mumbled to himself. From the next cubicle: "What's that?" Robert opened his desk drawer to look at his cheat sheet with the name of the new guy next door. Chris. That was it.

"Hey, Chris. Just commenting on August's numbers."

"Yeah, that was one swell month, wasn't it? I bet we'll hear good news about September's record pretty soon."

Robert couldn't care less about September's record. It was October 9th. His computer calendar had October 31st marked with MY PARTY in bold letters. He had clicked on "Yes" to accept the invite. There was not a "No" or "Maybe" option. His mandatory three-week vacation started tomorrow.

Robert remembered Halloween as a kid. The masks, the costumes, bags overflowing with candy. He knew there would be no candy in his bag this Halloween.

He walked down the corridor to the break room. Since he'd be leaving early, he took his lunch bag out of the refrigerator. *Might as well eat it now. LOL, Last Office Lunch*. Even now he had to make a joke of things.

When he returned to his desk, a cardboard box had materialized on it. Methodical as always, Robert filled the box with his few personal belongings.

His supervisor sauntered by and peered over Robert's cubicle. "I'm real sorry to see you go."

Robert looked into Jillian's green eyes and thought once again that she was one of the few women who could carry off lavender hair in a stylish butch cut.

"Thanks, Jillian. It's amazing how quickly the years fly by. Will I see you at my Party?"

"You bet. Take care, okay? See you soon." Jillian stuck her arm over the cubicle for a handshake, and Robert complied.

Chris popped his head up from his side. "Oh man, you're leaving already? I was just getting to know you!"

"Yeah, well, when 'They' say it's time to go, there's not much choice. Be glad you're young, Chris. I can't believe I'm 55 already."

"I'll try to make it to your Party."

"Thanks." Robert picked up his box and left the building. He didn't even bother to turn off his computer. While driving back to his small condo in the next town over, he remembered a Beatles' song that his maternal grandparents used to play when he was a kid. It was something about growing old, living in a cottage, grandchildren on the knees. He had forgotten the lyrics, so he hummed the catchy tune.

There was a beep at his wrist and a corresponding tone from the car's speakers. THE BEATLES, WHEN I'M SIXTY-FOUR, SERGEANT PEPPER'S LONELY HEARTS CLUB BAND, 1967 RECORDING. THE COST IS THREE COM COINS. APPROVE AND DOWNLOAD? YES OR NO.

Robert pushed 'Yes' on the dashboard and then wondered what was the point.

When he got home, he kicked the box into his hall closet and examined himself in the mirror on the closet door. Unlike the old man in the Beatles' song, he had a full head of brown hair, only a bit of white at the temples. A few wrinkles on his pale, clean-shaven face. His hazel eyes looked sad, and a bit scared. *I'm still fairly trim*, he thought. *I'm gonna ditch these stupid office clothes and wear nothing but shorts and a T-shirt until my party.*

Robert took a cold one to his balcony and sank into a rickety chaise lounge. There was nothing and nobody in his life. The cat he had for twenty years died last year. He hadn't had a girlfriend or gone on a date in at least two years. It was just as well, now that he was 55.

He leaned back, thinking. It was weird, what had happened in the USA. Conservative politics and religion had combined forces so birth control and abortions were things of the past. You couldn't even buy condoms without a doctor's prescription, but who could afford to visit a doctor? The population had soared.

There were too many people using up too many scarce resources. So, the government created The Party. If you were an average person, not somebody valuable, you got a Party during your 55th year.

Robert was average. He was pretty smart, a dedicated worker, didn't screw up much, but he had to go. He had been to some Parties and he knew that after a few hours, the person of honor disappeared, and that was that. Everyone else straggled out, usually quite inebriated or high, went home, and tried not to think too hard about when it would be their turn.

The rumor was that the person of honor was heavily drugged and taken away, euthanized, and then cremated. Only big shots got funerals and gravestones.

Robert's parents had their Party together with several friends who were the same age. At that time, Parties were held when you turned 60. Robert had hugged his parents, told them he loved them, and thanked them for everything. There were tears, but there was also music, dancing and laughter. Then . . . he didn't see his parents leave.

Robert suspected all the drinks were drugged.

During his three-week vacation, Robert imbibed a lot of beer. He put his condo on the market. He decided who would inherit the proceeds from the sale and also benefit from his Com Coin account and the liquidation sale of his belongings, such as his car. He was lucky to have all these possessions. Most people had to rent. He got his parents' condo—after their Party.

He decided to give everything to Rose. He hoped it would be a nice surprise for her and help her remember him. They'd stayed friends after they split up three years ago. She was 45, plenty of time to enjoy a bit of fortune.

The three weeks sped by quickly and then it was the 31st. A beep at his wrist. *TIME TO PARTY!*

Robert put on jeans and a vintage Wu-Tang Clan T-shirt and pulled on new cowboy boots. Maybe if he looked younger and more hip, people would feel sorry for him and . . . *and then complain to the President?*

"Yeah, right." Robert rolled his eyes at his own sarcasm. Rebellion was not an option.

He saw some little ghosts, mummies, and monsters trick-or-treating on the street. It was creepy how the government decided to throw his Party on Halloween. It was also unnerving how they knew his favorite restaurant. He and Rose used to frequent *La Cucina Italiana*; even after they broke up, Robert would walk down there a few times a month for a glass of red wine and whatever special they had going on.

Robert grimaced as he came face to face with his framed photo placed on an easel by the entrance to the banquet room. There was a full bar and the area was set up so guests could stand and mingle or sit at one of the little tables scattered around for more intimate conversations.

There was also a small dance floor. A handful of people were already dancing to the music, soft jazz and oldies. Waiters in formal black and white attire, looking like penguins, kept plenty of hors d'oeuvres coming.

Robert couldn't help thinking, *Well, at least some of the staff are wearing costumes.*

His heart pounded hard as he greeted colleagues at the bar. Robert's favorite brew, a British bitter called Flowers, was on hand.

Again, he wondered how "They" knew. He tasted the dark brew in his pint glass— *Was it different? Was it already drugged?*

Robert saw Jillian and Chris having a tête-à-tête in a corner of the room. *Was Chris being promoted to his former job right on the spot?* He felt the blood drain from his face and he clenched his teeth.

A fresh pint materialized in his hand. He couldn't remember getting it himself. While drowning his sorrowful rage with long swallows, his gaze fell on Rose. She was sitting alone with her head down, doodling circles with her index finger in the moisture her stemmed martini glass had left on the table.

"Rose! So great to see you!" Robert bent to hug her, doing his best not to spill his ale, and sat in the empty chair next to her.

Rose's sapphire eyes were rimmed in red. "Oh, Robert, I never thought this day would come. I am so sorry. We should have done more together." She ran her hands through her auburn hair, disheveling a loose bun already in danger of coming undone, and dabbed a tissue to her eyes.

Robert thought she looked glorious in her simple chemise. A tiny embroidered nosegay decorated her breast pocket. He wanted to touch it.

"Ah, Rose—you know all the reasons." Robert laid a hand over Rose's wet index finger. "It's hard to get close to anyone anymore. All that pie in the sky about getting married and having a family—it just wasn't for us. Don't feel bad, it's better this way. Here, let's get you another drink."

He hailed a penguin—*the guy really looked like an honest-to-God penguin*—and got Rose a refill of her gin martini. He knew her favorite drink. *Dry, straight up, with an olive.* Another pint arrived with the martini.

Robert lifted Rose's hand and gave it a squeeze. "Rose, I want you to know I've left everything to you—my car, what I got from the condo sale, my Com Coin account—everything."

Rose's eyes widened and she sat back in her chair.

"You mean so much to me, always have, and you're a lot younger, and, and . . . I want you to enjoy the time you have left." His face broke into a sloppy grin. "Happy Halloween!"

Rose let go of Robert's hand and furrowed her brow. "Halloween? Really? Robert, are you serious?"

Robert stood. "Yes, Rose, I am serious, and it's all taken care of. So, won't you do me the honor of this dance?"

With a short sigh, Rose nodded and followed Robert to the dance floor.

They held each other and swayed to a rendition of "Moon River." Others joined in, patting Robert on the back and crowding around him. His arm around Rose's waist, Robert was surrounded by a group of admirers, all holding up their glasses in a toast. Everyone appeared flushed and happy, relaxed even.

He was dancing with a real rose. She smelled wonderful and looked so pretty. He was in a beautiful oasis of flowers, all turning their sunny faces toward him.

"I love you all!" he roared.

"We love you, too!" The group pulsated to an unheard tune, a vibrating entity of laughing, happy, sighing, and loving human beings. The sensation lasted a long time.

The music came up again. This time, it was that old Joni Mitchell song, "Woodstock." Robert knew then what he had known all along, deep down. He was stardust. He was golden. He was one with everyth—

The Rustle of Black Silk

by Aletheia Morden

In those dreary days of post-World War II when parts of England lay in ruins and refugees roamed Europe, my mother and I lived in my grandmother's house full of heavy Victorian furniture and stern portraits. Mother went to work each morning as part of a much-needed work force. Money was in short supply in most households. A lot of the population was dead; too many men had a jacket sleeve or trouser leg neatly pinned where a limb had once been. I longed to go to school, but at four years old I had to wait another year for kindergarten.

Mornings were for housework until eleven o'clock when my grandmother would announce, "Time for a dance." We'd put our dusting rags down, pick up the hem of our skirts, and skip around to music on the radio. Ivor Novello's "We'll Gather Lilacs In The Spring Again" was a waltz. Then it would be time for lunch before those long, dreadful afternoons.

In winter it would be dark by four o'clock. We'd sit in the parlor: my grandmother in her high-backed chair next to the table by the window; me on an old kitchen chair with the legs sawn down so that my feet could touch the floor, playing with my doll by the fire. I loved the fire. Orange flames dancing in a frenzy, crackling and whispering secrets from long ago as the black coals turned red, then ashen gray, while little yellow stars twinkled on the soot hanging down from the chimney flue. My doll, Betty, loved it, too. She'd sit on my lap, nice and warm as the day shortened and purple shadows crept from the corners of the room.

Then a snap of starched white tablecloth on the parlor table, the clatter of china plates and silver utensils, the whistle of the teakettle in the scullery, and the sound of boiling water pouring over tea leaves in the flowered teapot. My grandmother's footsteps as she fetched cheese and margarine from the pantry—nobody had butter in those days.

Teatime.

She'd hand me a plate of bread and the long-handled toasting fork with three prongs. I'd impale a slice of bread and thrust it near the flames to toast as grandmother sat back down in her chair. Soon, she'd start to hum, softly at first, then louder as she beat time on the tablecloth with the cheese knife.

And then, "Don't burn the bread, Emily," grandmother would admonish, my name lost as she summoned that of her little sister, long-ago grown and gone to Canada.

"Don't worry, Betty," I'd whisper to my doll. "It will be all right."

I kept my back to the room, toasting slices of bread until the plate was full, each piece a little blackened around the three holes where the fork tines had been, evoking two eyes and a mouth. And then...and then...the swish of the baize curtain on its brass rail that led to the dark space under the stairs, the space where grandmother had slept every night during the war while bombs flew overhead, the space full of dark dreams.

"Mustn't look," I whispered to Betty as *They* came into the room. A smell of faded violets, the rustle of black silk from great-grandmother's Victorian skirt as *They* glided behind me to the tea table. Grandmother had summoned her long-ago dead parents. I had my doll and grandmother had hers. And grandmother was very, very angry with her dolls. She listed their transgressions: *His* for drunkenness and neglect, leaving them penniless. *Hers* for abandonment of mothering. Grandmother shouted curses, screaming "you'll burn in hell," as shadows danced over the walls and sparks flew up the chimney.

I held my dolly tight. "Good girl," I whispered to Betty. "Don't cry."

And then…and then…the front door slamming, my mother's high heels tapping down the hallway, home from her typing job at Ocean Insurance. The rustle of black silk, the swish of the baize curtain, the smell of violets fading as grandmother put her dolls away. Silence in the parlor save for the ticking of the old clock. My mother entering in her business suit, switching on the light, patting her hair in place, sitting down at the table and smiling at us.

"What's for tea, then?"

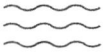

Life in a Vermont Artist's Colony

by Lois Requist

I've come here to write. Can I do it? Out my window in Bivins One, I note the pale overcast sky and grass sloping down toward a line of trees. It's autumn. Fallen leaves gather, lacking the weight or power to slide, waiting for a puff of wind to carry them to a new place. I am holding on to green and gold. Most of it will go away. The sky will darken, the air turn colder.

I left California for this? From my plain but adequate room, I wonder why I am here, and if, and if. In my ear, Roger Whittaker is singing, "Will the last word ever spoken be why?" Having "a room of one's own" and nothing to do but write—I may collapse under the weight of that responsibility.

I will think up characters—one strident, brisk, and unsettled, with a serious face and purpose, another a companion to sit in the room with me at night when the cold seeps inside my joints and muscles. That chill could steal my soul, if such a thing exists, and worse yet, steal the words I had intended to use for some extraordinary purpose.

When I come back from breakfast, there's a guy named Harry sitting on my bed. His long legs are stretched out in front of him.

I can't walk past. He's a long, tall drink of water. Not bad looking, either. 'Bout my age. Hmm... Wants to be a character in a novel.

It's not going to work out with him.

Harry drove over from the coast. Heard I needed people in my stories. Thinks he has what it takes. Traveled around the world on a tramp steamer thirty years ago. Imprisoned in Borneo in the worst conditions. Fought as a mercenary a few times. (Who would do that?) Has an ugly scar near one ear and can't remember how he got it. He's had relationships, too. Thinks he has a son in Hong Kong he's never seen.

Here we are—an interesting character and I can't use him.

"Why not?" he asks.

It's nothing personal. This is about me, not you. I have a brother named Harry, so I can't have a character by that name. The fictitious and the real would get mixed up. Just wouldn't work.

So, here I am…alone again. I find something wrong with every man, but that's another story.

I will draw several people, so I can talk to whoever interests me at the moment, though I am ill prepared for guests. I hope they won't expect food. All I have is bottled water and no glasses.

I could take them to one of the public rooms, but…complications would set in. Introductions become necessary.

So, what can I say about Jeffrey? Isn't he handsome? Yes, he's rather full of himself. Did I give him too much hair? He spends so much time moussing it, he doesn't have time to develop real character. He likes to sit on that barstool in the corner of the Burberry Peninsula Pub, so each person who enters sees his hair and its reflection in the mirror behind the bar.

I pause. Everyone looks at Jeffrey, at his hair that stands a full five inches above his scalp and maybe twelve inches wide above his temples, something dug up from an ancient and mysterious past, 10,287 BC. The plains of Africa. A small haystack.

He sleeps with a special neck pillow that elevates his head. I didn't mean for the hair to become a big deal, but I'm not fully in charge here. I was trying to differentiate him from Ronald, a baby

boomer in his 50s who has thin, wispy hair that drifts ineffectu-
ally across the bald spot on his head like a cow munching its way
across pasture.

Ronald knows the importance of things besides hair.

"Call me Ron," he says above the cell phone attached to one
side of his face. He's a wheeler-dealer, strictly left-brain, currently
day-trading on the Internet. Buy low. Sell high. He pays close attention to small movements because high and low need not be far
apart. He lives in Las Vegas and prides himself on never making
a business decision based on emotion. "Look at the numbers," he
says. When Joe and the other guys were putting serious money
down on Dallas, he stayed cool and out of it.

For his other needs, he is friendly with some of the highest paid
call girls on The Strip. Cindy Lou, a name borrowed from a Dr.
Seuss character, a member of the Who Family, gives him a deal.
Extra time thrown in or a freebie now and then. He shares tips on
the market with her.

"I happen to know…BJL is goin' up next coupla' days. Better get
your sweet ass down there and get some. Talked to this guy the
other night…he 'shouldn't a' been talkin', but ya know how it is…
the human animal is born with his mouth open and most never
learn to keep it shut. Had a few pops and god knows what else."

"You rely on a screw-off like that?"

"Gotta know your screw-offs. This one I know. And he owes
me…don't ask."

"I never ask… First thing in the morning, I'll make the call. You
haven't let me down yet," Cindy Lou says, taking a hit from the
joint they had rolled. She brought some of the good stuff with her
from what she grows, just enough for her own social needs. She
also grows orchids, not easy to do in a hot, dry climate, and African
violets. She's a member of the Las Vegas Call Girls Garden Club.
You have to be invited to join.

A horticulturist of sorts, she has turned her mother on to growing marijuana, so her mother lives comfortably now. Better than
social security and more reliable, as Cindy Lou hears it.

When Cindy Lou was growing up, her mother told her that she could be anything she wanted—president, a computer geek, lawyer, or even a queen, if she could find a country that had need of a queen. There are always conditions. Cindy Lou graduated summa cum laude from Princeton.

Why, then, did she end up in the world's oldest profession? Follow your bliss, she was advised. Some contend that farming is the oldest work. With Cindy Lou's green thumb, she is in either case deeply rooted to culture's oldest traditions.

Ever since that roll in the barn with Jose when she emerged with pieces of hay hanging in her hair, she knew what she liked. She soon realized how to reach the top of the profession quickly. No glass ceiling here. Make a man happy for…thirty seconds, and he is your slave for life…if you don't hang around asking if, and if, and why.

~~~~~

Out my window, the air has stopped moving. Nothing stirs. I wonder if life is frozen, the way my computer is sometimes, refusing all input, output, or access.

I need more substantive characters. Let's try a name like… Gertrude Bartholomew. She cannot be trivial. Cindy Lou's profession is probably not an option. A schoolteacher? Plain clothes and no makeup. Oh, please don't be so stereotypical. Why not? She is from Wisconsin, goes to church, sings in the choir, and eats cheese.

"That's not what I want out of life. Call me Trudi. Right there, you drop half that baggage. Speaking of baggage…" Trudi looks around the room. "Where do I put my things?"

You can't stay here. It's not allowed.

"I traveled all this way for nothing!"

Hey, I'm only here by the skin of my…words. It's a single bed. Set your bag down. You can stay for a bit.

"You can do quite a bit with a single bed," Cindy Lou says.

"And exactly who are you?" Trudi demands.

I introduce Jeffrey, Ron, and Cindy Lou Who.

"Where are you guys staying?" Trudi, with reddish brown hair and a thickly freckled face, asks. She wears calf-high brown boots, leggings, a short plaid skirt and a gold sweater.

Trudi stands in a dim light. I bring her in closer to the writing table and pull the arm of the lamp out to see her full and lively face, and something else that I recognize and need—the direct look in those gray-green eyes. She has loved and been touched by it—been left and bruised by that as well. I'm starting to get it right—she is three-dimensional.

The others need more work—more suffering, perhaps.

"We don't want to suffer," they sing in unison. "Suffer, suffer, suffer, no more suffering down here, oh yeah."

I look them over.

Jeffrey's hair has more than one dimension, but the rest of him is scrawny.

You need to work out, Jeffrey. Pump some iron.

"What about my hair? Won't it get all...sweaty and stuff?"

"Look man, get over the hair," Ron says.

"I kind of like it," says Cindy Lou.

"And I thought you had good taste in men," Ron says.

This is like creating children—you never know how it will turn out.

A feeling of pathos comes over me.

"So what's happening?" Ron asks.

"My father is dying," Trudi says without a quiver of the lower lip. "He knows and accepts it. He's 72. He's had a good life. Mother has enough money. It is the rest of us who don't know where to look or what to do or how to be in the face of death."

Jeffrey pats his hair and looks embarrassed. "You have...nice hair."

Ron smiles. "Does he have a will? A living trust? I can get you a deal...the death and dying package. Attorney I know. "

"Have you talked to Hospice?" Cindy asks.

"My mother died four years ago," Jeffrey says. "It was sudden. A heart attack. My father and I have never talked about it. Never (even?) said her name."

"Never?" says Cindy.

"It seems like you would want to say her name," Trudi says to Jeffrey.

"Yes, you know, I do. I want to remember her out loud, not just inside. She used to walk down to the corner where I got off the school bus. I would see her standing there, her thick, dark brown hair tied loosely at the back of her neck—that must be where mine came from—waving as I got off, smiling as I came running toward her, taking my hand, walking the half-block to the house, just glad to be together."

"And her name?" Cindy asks.

"Mary Louise," Jeffrey says. "Mother."

There is silence then. After a while, Jeffrey turns to Trudi and says, "Tell me about your father."

"I'm outta here," Ron says. "I got stuff to do."

You don't leave until I say you leave.

"Whoa…what's this…a prison cell?"

No. I was just hoping you would hang around until…

"Until what?"

Until I get to know you better.

"What's to know? What you see is what you get. If you are look-ing for depth or anything, you got the wrong guy."

"He's not quite as tough as he sounds," Cindy Lou says. "He doesn't know any other way to be, gets uncomfortable with these heavy subjects. I do, too. I've never lost anyone." She turns toward Trudi. "There's just my mom. Never knew my dad. Never been close to any man."

Ron laughs.

"You know what I mean," she goes on, "really know them, so you could, like, call them if you needed to talk or something."

"You could call me," Ron says, looking away. "If you could get through." A pause. "You could leave a message. I'd get back to you at the end of the trading day." Again, he stops. "I could call before that." He says it slow, as if while walking across the grass he spots something lying there—a piece of himself—and decides to pick it up.

Out my window, the leaves are still or lightly undulating. One hanging leaf, however, has caught the wind, is dancing madly, a full-body ecstasy, in the long, late afternoon sun. I want my life to be like that.

~~~~~

Harry is here, again, when I get back from breakfast.

"My middle name is Samuel. I could be Sam," he offers.

Ah-h. I'll have to think about that. Leave your card and résumé.

"Not that! I hate that!" Harry says, and his broad shoulders quiver. "It's like…leaving a part of me behind with someone who doesn't know or care about me."

I hate being described like that, but you are interrupting my flow…wait out in the hall a minute please, while I begin this where I had intended to. I need to see out my window, to read the mood of the sky and what weather is arriving. What happens next? It's crowded here, with the various characters, their misdeeds and grandparents.

Jeffrey has hired a personal trainer and is moving in workout equipment. Where are we going to put it? I don't think people in Vermont sweat; at least I find it difficult to perspire here. Vermonters have learned to hold any extra body heat they generate in reserve for those days when the wind-chill factor is numbing. *I suggested exercising, Jeffrey, but maybe it's not such a good idea. We'll have to go to Santa Barbara, where you see skin—on the street— and most of it is tan and in good shape. You could work out with my son.*

"A trip! When do we go? I'll have to fix my hair…" Jeffrey says. "Do you love him more than me?"

Y-yes. He's been in my life longer, and…he's my son.

"But, I'm your creation as well," Jeffrey says, wringing his hands.

I'm wondering how long Jeffrey will be around. He understands my reservations, but decides to take a chance, work out, and hope for the best. I note his perceptivity.

"I'm even willing to suffer," Jeffrey says, "If it's not too bad, you know, and doesn't last too long and doesn't really hurt."

Ron sneers. "You wimp," he says, "Not me. I'm busy anyway, so if this character thing causes actual pain, I'm on the first bus out of town."

"They are still waiting for the first bus in town," Trudi says.

~~~~~~

A sculptor, a writer, and a painter are here from Japan with limited English. The sculptor turns to Ron.

"We went to the grocery store. We asked the clerk, 'Where do we catch the bus?' She laughed. We said, 'A taxi. Where do we get a taxi?' She laughed bigger."

"You are here to work," Trudi says. She gestures to the personal trainer. "Are you going to get him started on a program?"

Trudi, just because I brought you in to be a substantial character doesn't mean you have to play the heavy. Still, I would like a quiet evening with her, a little wine and good conversation. Inquiring minds want to know if and if and why.

She has started a conversation with the personal trainer, now dubbed PT and then—why not?—Barnum. Now, Trudi is lifting weights, all spandex and sweat, while people keep asking me when the circus opens. They've seen the big-rigs pull in, and the children at the grade school are excited. I think things have gotten out of hand...and Harry...Sam still waiting in the hall.

"Maybe I could have more than three dimensions," Trudi says. "Anyway, I'm way ahead of you guys with three."

"Well," Cindy says, "No one ever accused me of being flat..."

"Dearie," Trudi says, "it's about depth, and you don't become deep…in your chosen profession."

"So, I bet I've read more heavy books than you," Cindy says.

"Go to a food kitchen, or volunteer to help someone out. You need experience…of a different kind," Trudi says. Cindy puts on her coat and goes out.

Take Harry with you, I holler. Is that a good idea—putting those two together?

~~~~~

I walk to the Lecture Hall that used to be a church before it was the Town Hall and Opera House. Built in 1832, it has experienced decay and restoration. The old churches are now art studios. I wonder where and if the saints are marching now. I leave soon. Cindy and Harry/Sam are walking by, arm in arm. They nod briefly to me. I don't think he cares about the character thing anymore. Unreliable. Inconstant. Philanderer.

At the Plum & Main Restaurant, Harry/Sam and Cindy are huddled in a booth for two. I sit at the counter, order hot mulled cider. That gone, I return to my temporary home. Darkness and the lost souls have gathered outside my window and peer in at me, seeking a plotline, a place to reside. I reach for something to hold on to. The poet, Charles Wright, wrote: "Darkness is only light that hasn't reached us yet."

Out my window is Johnson, Vermont, what some might call a "one horse town," though I haven't seen one. No traffic lights.

I need a real cup of coffee, Trudi. Come with me.

"I didn't bring snow boots," Trudi says. "Bring me back a double latte, half decaf, non-fat milk, no foam, with cinnamon and chocolate on top."

She has to be so complex about everything.

"Double espresso here," Ron and Jeffrey say together. After lifting three-pound weights for his biceps, Jeffrey's forehead is beaded in sweat. Ron's fingers tap on the computer. Harry (Sam) is drunk and cursing in the corner, getting into the right place to be…himself. It's all that roving, a lack of family ties, or a permanent address. I'll have to get him to AA.

"Don't try to clean him up," Trudi says. "He's just what you need—for conflict and a love interest. We're all figments of your imagination, anyway."

Jeffrey shudders. "I don't want to be a figment."

"Don't go changin', tryin' to please me," Cindy torches. "I love you just the way you are."

I'll need that computer when I get back, I say to Ron.

"Could you work nights? When the market is closed?" He asks.

I'm afraid not. Without resolving our dueling needs, I cross the bridge and walk to Main Street and the French Press Cafe, which is not a coffee shop in the traditional sense, but in the *au courant* mode. Steam hisses, and latte, cappuccino, and espresso are tossed around like words that have always been in our vocabulary, and not, in fact, interlopers with French-Italian backgrounds, carrying green cards…or not. It is wise, especially in California, to follow Cindy's practice and not ask.

At the French Press Café, a sign on the wall says, "Due to the occasional uncertainty between the cyclic and linear nature of the passage of time, 'our reduced-price refill' option is defined to expire at the end of the stay during which the regular cup of coffee is purchased."

I take the drinks back with an extra double espresso for Harry. Since there is no space for me, I go back downtown, walk past one- and two-story traditional clapboard houses of white, gray, yellow, red, or blue. Some have porches. A light purple and pink two-story house atop a hill puts me in mind of Norman Bates. The blue one across from the gas station has lace curtains. Only the architecture of the Mechanics Bank hints of the 20th century.

"Visible Layers of Time: A Perspective on the History and Architecture of Johnson, Vermont" says there has been a settlement here for 5000 years. Surrounded by the Green Mountains, the village sits in a pocket formed by the Lamoille and Gihon

Rivers. Highway 15, Main Street, carries most of the traffic into and escaping from this ideal place to do one's art.

In Johnson's Pharmacy, I look for Harper's Magazine. Bob, a visiting writer, dropped off certain words, and I want to pass some of those along to people in California.

"You probably can't buy Harper's in all of Vermont," a resident says. I check next door at the Grand Union, a grocery store. I have no need to buy food here, but wine is necessary.

"Not bad for a cheap wine," the clerk says when I buy an $8 Merlot.

"Well, it's not the cheapest."

"I'm used to $80 wine," she says.

What is this world coming to? The grocery clerk drinks $80 wine!

"Do you have a mousepad?" I say to the man behind the till at Beard's Hardware.

"A mousetrap?" he asks, his small gray head looking uncomprehendingly at me.

"No? Never mind. How about a nine-volt battery?"

"What did you want?"

"A nine-volt battery."

"No, the other thing," he says.

"A mousepad."

For nearly a century, Beard's Hardware has been in business, and the mouse has been an enemy. This man wonders if I want to provide aid and comfort to the hunted. He sells me the battery reluctantly and eyes me suspiciously until I leave.

Trudi and I eat at the Red Mill, which sits almost in the Gihon River. A gristmill for 135 years; beginning in 1785, flax and wheat were ground here and sold to the community. Grist—according to *Merriam-Webster's Dictionary* (Tenth Edition, Updated Annually, "The words you need today")—disappointing that I did not learn this until the 46th day of my 53-day stay—"Grist" could be grain, or "the basis of a story," or "something turned to advantage."

～～～～～

We have heard gunshots in recent weeks, an incongruous sound in this safe sanctuary. Early on Saturday morning, I walk to Tangles Salon for a haircut. A pickup truck passes with a freshly killed deer splayed across the hood.

~~~~~~

The Center is designed to be "non-competitive and non-hierarchical," but we bring those things with us, stuffed in the little pockets on the sides of our suitcases.

Since arriving, Ron sees art as an investment, so he asks artists quietly, "Whose work do you like? What is it worth? Any good artists who are likely to die soon?" Many artists sidle up to him.

Ron, Cindy, Trudi, and I walk to Johnson State College, a twenty-minute climb the long way. Jeffrey has worked out and is exhausted. We stand on the steps of the Shape Center looking across the valley at the surrounding Green Mountains against the pale winter sky. If I were an artist, I would draw these barren trees with dark centers that feather out to less but higher, the intermingling branches. The grove there, on the distant hill with the sun behind it.

Trudi finds the library and wanders through fiction, nodding at Stegner, Vidal, Wolfe, and Woolf. It's hard to choose from among the worlds drawn between those covers. Cindy admires the three-story tall windows, then settles down to read the Boston Globe. Ron embraces a computer.

We walk down the hill to the covered Power House Bridge. Built in 1872, it crosses the Gihon River. In cold weather, the water's edges glaze over. When it rains, the river rushes. Folks still talk about the flood of 1927, the drowned family, and the many homeless.

Cindy wants a picture, so we pose, take turns clicking. How many faces will show up in the photo? Will the images of Ron, Trudi, and Cindy be clear? They're figments of my imagination!

There is so little here, according to the map, but I can't contain all that is in Johnson, Vermont.

~~~~~

Snow is falling again. My mind bent on leaving, I wonder what of my experiences here will stay with me?

Harry (Sam) has disappeared on his own, will probably roam the earth always seeking something that is at the next destination. Cindy and Ron leave on the same flight from Burlington for Las Vegas. I wonder if either of them will continue exactly as before or whether the experience here will stretch their world.

Jeffrey has been accepted as an artist in the next session, so he will stay, taking space in the sculpture studio because he does not paint, and where else can you put someone whose body is his art?

"Hey—I'm just as good as you, Trudi," he gloats.

"Well," she says, but stops, not wanting to deprecate his position or the self-confidence he has gained from it. Tough, but kind, that is what I have always admired in her.

Bach Don, who is from Vietnam, sells me a painting. Her landscape of Vermont. She does not know what price to ask. "I give it away at home," she says.

Ann, a painter, who lives on an island off the coast of Maine, says, "When I go home, I might be the constable. I won't drive a car or carry a gun, but I may put a blue light on my bicycle helmet."

I am left with that melancholy feeling I have at the end of anything.

Trudi and I are picked up for the four-hour drive to Manchester. Snow is falling, sticking in the trees and on the roofs of the clapboard houses in rural Vermont. Stowe is a picture postcard.

Trudi starts to walk toward another gate.

Wait! Wait! I call. *You need to go home with me! I can use you!*

"Really? All right then! What about Jeffrey and Cindy Lou?" She asks.

Perhaps. I can reach them if needed.

Out my window, the Manchester Airport looms. I open my purse. Notes of all kinds are there. I throw out the notes about local stuff in Johnson. The rest stay with me.

~~~~~

Winter Song

by Nicky Ruxton

Dust swirls in a stream of pre-dawn light. Hunching over my writing table, I find no position that brings relief. My bones tense in familiar ways as morning crests over the wooded hills outside. The pen lies mute after another restless night. Staring out the attic window, I watch silhouetted wrens gather on bare branches. The natural world, oblivious to my discomforts, doesn't judge my jumbled thoughts, or crumpled appearance. I clench a pearl-blue shawl, the one my mother knit for herself, around my shoulders, its open weave too thin to assuage my distress or defend against melancholy's hold.

Watching birds flap and preen, I hear my mother's voice, "If you can't say anything nice, dear, don't say anything at all." She repeated that phrase often, but I was immune to listening when living under her roof. It later proved a valuable lesson.

Do these winter wrens cackle with kindness, or do they mock the way I used to? My mother had a simple approach to life and maintained a respectful distance, the way birds do, spreading across branch or wire. I used up all the space she gave me to spread my wings, but somehow, I needed more—and flew away.

Shivering, I stretch the woolen shawl tighter around me. I fasten it with a binder clip to free my hands, to rub away the chill of longing. The signs of arthritis are more noticeable when I don't write, stiffening from an untended imagination.

In these quiet hours, regrets are my prison. Mother sits in a rocking chair beside my writing table. She coos words of encouragement, like a mama bird atop a twiggy nest, filling me with hope for a better life—better than the one she had.

In my youthful haste and rebellion, I migrated one winter, immune to her cooing.

As I close my eyes against the rising light, memories press the soft edges of my sorrow. Cradling my head in the crook of shawled arms, I rock and hear my mother whisper, "Hush, little baby," which lifts the tired from my bones, for moments that are never long enough.

Perhaps sleep will return and then my pen will take flight, scattering word seeds over the horizon of my reshaped thoughts. Mother's voice fades with the coming of day, but she'll return to fill me with another winter song.

Samhain Eve

by Marty Malin

It's the first of October and I'm having those urges again. An increasingly pressing need to make plans, to spend my birthday away from home. I can't tell you exactly why. It's always been this way, for as long as I can remember.

My wife Justine doesn't understand this. I don't really understand it either.

"You're creeping me out, Mitch," Justine said. "There's something going on here and either you won't let me in on your little secret, in which case why not just tell me to mind my own business, or you've blown a circuit board." Justine's working on her bachelor's degree in electrical engineering, so she often uses such images.

My psychiatrist, Dr. Morgan, is trying to help both of us understand, but she's clearly fumbling in the dark, looking at pages in my family album that Justine has tabbed with colorful Post-it arrows. Dr. Morgan seems a bit flummoxed as she looks through the album. The pages Justine has marked with the Post-its are my birthday photos, 8 x 10 photos of me and my parents, from the time I was one year old until I turned eighteen last year. We're always holding hands in a circle, in front of an open fire, our faces raised to the sky.

And we're naked. Skyclad, as my parents used to call it. I'm mildly embarrassed, wondering how Dr. Morgan will react to seeing me in my birthday suit.

Maybe I don't need to worry. The reason we're in Dr. Morgan's office is that Justine can't see the pictures. Or rather, Justine thinks there aren't any pictures. She's betting Dr. Morgan won't see any pictures either.

"What's going on, Mitch?" Justine asked when I showed her the album. "Your birthday pages have nothing on them. They're blank. Why are you telling me they have pictures of you and your parents?"

"What do you mean no pictures? There are eighteen of them, one for every birthday celebration I ever had."

"Mitch, I'm telling you there's absolutely nothing on those pages. Nothing. They're blank. There are no pictures. Not even any mounting corners on the album pages, like the other photos in the album. Nothing: zip, zilch, nada. You're seeing things that aren't there. Either that or you're trying to be funny. Which, by the way, you aren't, so cut it out."

I insisted there were eighteen large photos. What was wrong with her?

"We need to get you some help, Mitch" she said finally. "Maybe this has something to do with the upcoming anniversary of your parents' death, or disappearance, or whatever the hell happened to them."

And that's how we ended up here with Dr. Morgan. Allow me to tell you a little more of my story while Dr. Morgan is pondering what might be going on.

Ever since I can remember, my parents and I have gone on vacation toward the end of October. My parents called it my "birthday vacation." That seems logical since I was born on October 31, in the year of our Lord 2000.

Halloween. Or, as my parents called it, *Samhain Eve*. They explained that Halloween's a Christian version of the ancient Gaelic festival of *Samhain* with its ritual fires, seasonal foods and prayers. Most people think the fires are for chasing away ghosts. My parents said most people are wrong about that, as most people are wrong about almost everything.

My parents said we light fires on *Samhain Eve* to welcome the spirits of our ancestors on the night when the veil between the living and the dead is as sheer as a spiderweb. We're not trying to scare them away. We're helping them find us. The ancestors come looking for us on *Samhain Eve* to reassure us, to bless us and quiet our fears about death.

My parents chanted *Samhain Eve* prayers on my birthday, but they did not teach them to me. I never saw any ancestors either, but I knew they were there. My parents said I would understand more when I became a man, but for now, all I needed to know was that my family loved me, and the ancestors also love and protect me.

I will explain all of this to Dr. Morgan when she finishes looking at the album. I don't know if she will understand any better than my wife, but it's the least I can do for her. I may tease her sometimes, but Dr. Morgan's been an absolute godsend.

I don't know for certain what happened to my parents, but they are probably now among the ancestors. We were on vacation last October as usual, somewhere in the South American rain forest, in Paraguay, I think. My parents simply disappeared into the jungle the day after my eighteenth birthday. The Guarani Indians who were celebrating with us told me my parents went dancing with the spirits.

Justine and I were engaged to be married soon so her family took me in while I wrestled with the loss of my mom and dad. Justine's parents were the ones who connected me with Dr. Morgan. With her help, I got well enough to follow through with our planned marriage in June.

Things were going fine until my October urge reared its head. That's when I dragged out the family album. I wanted to show Justine my pictures and explain our *Samhain Eve* tradition.

The first time my parents and I celebrated my *Samhain Eve* birthday together was when I was one year old. There I am in the picture, barely able to stand alone, the three of us holding hands in front of a huge bonfire. Mom said it was in Wyoming somewhere.

A couple of years ago, I asked my Dad who took these birthday photos. He and my mom just smiled. "We don't know," my mom said. "The photos just show up in the album. Likely, the ancestors have something to do with it."

I thought she was just repeating family lore. Dad must have had a remote-controlled camera rigged up somewhere.

I could never remember much about these celebrations, even when my parents and I leafed through the album together. Mom would say things like, "Remember this birthday when you turned ten and we stayed in that old castle in the Carpathians? You said you wanted to be a vampire when you grew up. Of course, we just laughed and explained there was no such thing."

Dr. Morgan looked up from the album. "Mitch, will you describe for me what you see on this page?" she asked, pointing to a page with a bright green sticky arrow.

"That's me and my parents on my fifth birthday. I think we were somewhere in Cabo, someplace like that."

Dr. Morgan and Justine looked at each other. Justine started to speak but Dr. Morgan silenced her with "that look."

"And this one?" Dr. Morgan asked, pointing to the page with the pink arrow.

"That's my seventeenth birthday," I said. "I think we were staying in a dacha outside St. Petersburg, but I don't remember much about that either."

I reached for Justine's hand. She was shaking. I moved closer and put my arm around her.

Dr. Morgan closed the album carefully. "I do not know how to explain this," she said, "but I believe Mitch *does* see pictures on those pages where you and I see nothing. I simply do not understand his ability to do so. But I'm not comfortable concluding that Mitch is hallucinating. He seems completely in touch with reality.

For the moment, it's likely best that we accept that he is seeing what he says he is seeing and just leave it at that."

"Well, I don't," said Justine, wiping tears from her eyes. "This is completely nuts."

"I could refer you to another psychiatrist for a second opinion, if you wish. But nobody is in any danger, so I don't think we need to be in a hurry about anything."

Justine and I looked at each other.

"Do you want me to see someone else, Honey?" I asked. "Because if you do, I will."

Justine shrugged her shoulders.

"Why don't we all do some more thinking about it," Dr. Morgan said. "I'll confer with a colleague, with your permission, and let's get back together next week and talk further. May I keep the album until then?"

The following week, when we went back to Dr. Morgan's office, she was her usual collected self.

"I've been talking with Dr. Chambliss down the hall. She's a trained anthropologist as well as a licensed psychologist and she has a lot of experience with shamanism and other cultural traditions. I thought we might walk over to her office together. Are you game?"

Dr. Chambliss' office was a museum of anthropological curiosities. Six-foot-high wooden tribal figures dominated the cavernous room. The walls were covered with elaborate fetishes and masks inlaid with shells and ivory. Museum cases, filled with exotic objects, rattles, jewelry and the odd skull were stationed around the room.

"Welcome," Dr. Chambliss said warmly, as we entered her office. "Pay no attention to all of this," she said, sweeping her arm around the room with a dismissive gesture. As if that were possible. The large desiccated crocodile lurking in one corner of the room seemed reason enough to pay attention. "Come, take a seat, be comfortable," she said, motioning us toward overstuffed chairs around a large low table in the center of the room. "Let me get some refreshments for everyone."

We waited in silence broken only by the ticking of a grandmother clock standing between two carved wooden figures with outsized phalluses while Dr. Chambliss retrieved a tea trolley from a nook and poured steaming cups of mint tea.

She settled into her chair. "So, what do we think?" she said conspiratorially after a few moments. "As Dr. Morgan knows, gifted people in many cultures see things other people can't see. And even in our own culture, as many as 3% of perfectly normal adults recall having unique perceptual experiences before the age of 21. We probably shouldn't call them hallucinations."

Dr. Morgan nodded her agreement.

"Let me ask you a question, Mitch. When your parents showed you these photos when you were younger, what did you think?"

"I enjoyed looking at them, but my father's explanation that the photos somehow magically appeared in the album and that the ancestors had something to do with it wasn't completely satisfying. So, on my seventeenth birthday, I vowed I would find that hidden camera somewhere. But I didn't find it.

"And on my eighteenth birthday, I tried again. I still didn't find any cameras but after I got back home from the jungle, I checked the album. The photo was there, just as I expected it would be. The only explanation that made sense was that the ancestors took the photo and put it in the album as they always had!"

Dr. Chambliss nodded. Dr. Morgan was as still as the statues along the wall.

"So, I promised to tell you what I think," Dr. Chambliss began. "I think there are images on that page that Mitch sees perfectly well, even if none of us can see them. In fact, I think *only* Mitch can see them now that his parents are no longer alive."

"That just can't be," Justine said, shaking her head in disbelief. "Either the photographs are real, and we can all see them, or they're not and Mitch can't see them either."

"But what if we postulate that they might not be photographs at all?" Dr. Chambliss said. "What if the ancestors have some different way of creating images? Images that were only meant for Mitch and his family to see?"

"Well, if that's the case, why can't I see them?" Justine said. "Mitch and I are family now and I can't see anything on those pages."

Dr. Chambliss nodded her head patiently. "What are your plans for Mitch's birthday this Halloween or, perhaps we should say, *Samhain Eve*?"

"Well, since Mitch's birthday tradition is obviously so important to him, I booked a house in the California high desert outside of Borrego Springs. There's a fire pit where he can do his birthday ritual, a hot tub and ..."

I interrupted excitedly, "*We* can celebrate my birthday."

"Right," Justine continued. "If Mitch wants us to get butt-nek-kid and hold hands by a fire, I'm game. What could it hurt? The stars should be beautiful in the high desert. It still feels kind of spooky, but if that's what Mitch wants, and you and Dr. Morgan don't think he's completely crackers, that's what we'll do."

"Sounds lovely," Dr. Chambliss said. "I'll be eager to hear all about it. For what it's worth, you'll be in good company.

Thousands of Wiccans, neopagans, and assorted others around the world will be celebrating *Samhain Eve* with their own prayers and ceremonies.

"Now, is there anything more I can do for you? Would you care for more tea?"

We politely declined.

The stars in the high desert *were* astonishingly beautiful. We had a spectacular view of the Milky Way. Maybe not all 400 billion stars and 100 billion planets but a slew of them.

Still, I was hesitant.

"What's wrong?" asked Justine.

"What if we're not supposed to do this? What if this was some-thing only my parents understood?"

"You're making way too big a deal about it, Mitch. It'll be fun, dancing around the firepit like a couple of naked savages. We'll probably freeze our asses off, but then we can get into our jammies and have hot cocoa and birthday cake."

"I don't know why I'm feeling like this. What if I get it wrong? I don't even know the prayers."

"Listen, Mitch, we don't have to do this if you don't want to. We can just go stargazing or we can stay inside and play Scrabble. What are you afraid of?"

"It's not that I'm afraid. It's another feeling entirely. No. I need to do this. *We* need to do this. Everything in my being is telling me that's what we need to do tonight."

I took Justine's hands. "Honey, do you think my parents will come tonight? I mean, the spirits of my parents?"

Justine was quiet for a moment. "I don't know how this is supposed to work, Mitch. You know I'm skeptical about the whole ancestor thing. But if this is something you need to do, and it looks to me like it is, I'll be there with you."

I went outside to light the bonfire. The Milky Way splashed the sky with light and color. It was breathtaking. I went back inside to get Justine.

"It's time," I told her.

"Mitch, it's barely eight o'clock. Shouldn't we wait until midnight?"

"I was born at 8:14 in the evening. This time seems right."

"Okay. What do we do?"

"Let's take off our clothes and go outside."

I drew her close and kissed her. She was trembling.

"Are you cold?" I asked.

"No," she answered. "I'm fine. Did I remember to tell you that I love you?"

I smiled and led her to the far side of the fire pit. The blazing flames warmed our backs.

"Look at the sky!" I said, taking her other hand, turning her gently to face me.

We held hands in silence. I don't know where it came from, but I started praying.

*Now is the night when the veil between
our world and the spirit world is thinnest.*

*Tonight is a night to welcome those who came before.
Tonight we honor the ancestors.*

*Spirits of our fathers and mothers, we call to you,
and welcome you to join us for this night.*

*You watch over us always,
protecting and guiding us,
and tonight we thank you, as we thank you always.*

*Your blood runs in our veins,
your spirits are in our hearts,
your memories are in our souls.*

*We remember all of you
and you live on within us
and within those who are yet to come.*

We turned to face the desert and the mountains beyond. And we began to see them. Thousands of them, old men and women, young men and women, adolescents, children, infants. And in front of the throng, my mom and dad.

I started to call out to them, but they shook their heads. Again, we stood silently, regarding one another across the distance, across the thinnest of veils. I felt a warmth like I used to experience when my parents and I performed this ritual, before they disappeared in the rain forest. Later, Justine would tell me she felt it too.

I don't know how long we stood there before the ancestors slowly dissolved into the desert night. And it was over. I drew Justine close to me.

"Did you see them?" I asked excitedly.

"Yes," she said, squeezing my hand. "Oh Mitch, I still can't believe it, but I just saw it, with my own eyes."

Suddenly she tugged at my hand. "Let's go back inside. I need to do something."

We went back into the house and Justine went into the bedroom to retrieve the album.

"I'm almost afraid to look, Mitch."

She sat beside me on the sofa and I opened the album. "Oh my God!" she said. "It's all there, just like you said. Look at that one. You're so cute, dancing all bare butt with your mom and dad."

We went through the pages one by one. I told her what I remembered about each birthday, which was everything. Unlike before, nothing was hazy. I remembered each celebration, each location.

There was a photo I hadn't seen before. Justine and me holding hands, skyclad, the fire at our backs, looking up into the sky. The ancestors had welcomed her into the family. We were loved and protected.

But there was something different about the photo and it took me a moment to see it. Justine saw it about the same time I did. There was a circle of light, about the size of a nickel, on Justine's abdomen, a couple of inches below her navel.

We looked at each other incredulously as it dawned on us what we were seeing.

Still, we were completely unprepared as we turned the page. Our hearts melted and we dissolved in laughter, shedding more than a few tears of joy, when we saw the face of our yet-to-be-born child.

The ancestors had written a name and birthdate below the photograph. But I'm a little superstitious, so I'm not going to reveal anything more.

Encounters

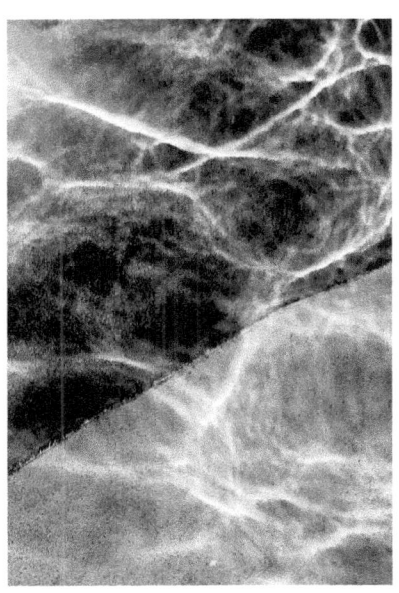

Crushed

by Nicky Ruxton

When I was seven years old, my great Auntie Ling came from China to live with us. Hunch-shouldered with an unsteady walk, her cracked-earth face was the hue of withered summer apricots. She smelled of wet tobacco and mentholated balm. We sipped lemon-ginseng tea together.

She showed me a pair of Chinese red silk slippers embroidered with phoenix birds and lotus blossoms. They were half the length of a yellow school pencil and threadbare. I wondered how dolls wore out their shoes.

Auntie said, "By you age, all girl in *lotus slipper*, marry best, good husband." I nodded, but I didn't understand why dolls needed slippers or husbands.

"Auntie Ling," I asked, "why did you save these old doll shoes?"

With moist almond eyes she replied, "No dolly. Lotus slipper for *new moon* feets."

When she removed her cotton socks I saw the truth of her crushed doll beauty.

~~~~~

ThumpThumpThump

by Deborah Morrison

Thumpthumpthump the footsteps pounded up the ramp to the classroom. I heard the sound and took a deep slow counting breath. 1......2.......3. By 4, the door was flung open and the voice boomed through the classroom, surprisingly loud coming from the smallest second grader on campus.

"I'mHereWhereIsEveryone?" The small boy rushed his words to match the quick flutter of his limbs. I only understood his words because I had known him since kindergarten. OK, here we go, I thought, breathing again 5......6......7.

"Good morning, Jordan. Seems like you're early for reading group. Want to help me set up?"

"OK," he said and proceeded to dash around the kidney shaped table, tossing seven workbooks and pencils. Workbooks and pencils screamed across and around the tabletop, most, amazingly, ending up close to where they needed to be. This workbook pencil frenzy happened so quickly I didn't have time to remind Jordan how many we needed.

"Oh, Jordan, remember it's only you and April for the reading group today. We only need two workbooks."

"Oh, OK," he said and shoved the extra workbooks towards one end of the table, some missing the mark and landing on the floor.

I did not react, knowing I had to pick my battles and focus on the positive through the time we would be working together. Any comment about workbook placement could shut him down into a sulky pile under the table. My priority for Jordan was to teach him to read, so all other minor happenings during our sessions were not important to me.

We both turned, not really hearing anything, but vaguely aware that something was shifting behind us. There is a heightened auditory awareness that comes when you live in the world of children. Jordan had this heightened sensitivity too. His was due to hyperactivity, mine was also probably due to hyperactivity, but also to years of tightly wound senses. Senses that knew having knowledge ahead of time was always a good thing in the world of the elementary school.

I found over time, I was always visually scanning my surroundings, keeping my ears tuned for slight changes in the sounds around me and my senses of touch, taste, and smell (think years of school cafeteria lunch smells wafting through your nostrils, years of yard duty filled with flailing limbs and screaming short people) had all "blossomed" since I began this special education teaching gig.

The sound we had both sensed was the door. No footsteps up the ramp had preceded its opening and April sort of drifted in, her eyes dreamy.

"Good morning, April," I said.

Long silence. I waited. Finally, as if she was waking from a good dream and realizing where she was, April said, "Oh, hi, Mrs. M." She smiled slowly and plunked herself down in her chair.

Jordan, still hovering in the vicinity of the table, looked at her and smiled.

"What's for snack? Do you have any of those brown wrinkly things from your lunch?" April asked. Jordan paused a brief second in his roaming to listen to my answer.

"I do. You really liked those prunes, I think." I placed a few on a napkin for them to share.

"Yay," they both shouted.

Food was the only thing I'd found to tempt Jordan to perch for a while at the table with us and to quiet the constant swirling that filled his small body, so it had become our daily reading group ritual. The snack always came out of my lunch bag. It was always something grabbed quickly off my cupboard shelf or plucked from the garden as I ran out the door each morning. This seemed to keep them a bit more interested than if I were to pass out the typical goldfish crackers or something they were more familiar with.

Today Jordan still had not sat down, but he reached for a prune, plopped it in his mouth, and remained in motion, working the prune around and around in his mouth, as his legs took him around and around the table. How he was able to talk with all this movement constantly amazed me.

"Wheredidyougetthese?Ilikethem," he called out.

"Safeway," I answered.

"REALLY?" He seemed dumbfounded for maybe the first time since I'd met him.

"OK, let's sit down and get started," I said. April had been quietly following Jordan with her eyes as she slowly enjoyed her prune.

"He moves a lot," she said.

"He has lots of energy," I said.

"Oh, that's why he moves so much." A small light-bulb moment had apparently been triggered by my simple answer and, satisfied with my explanation, she opened her workbook in a deliberate, business-like way.

Jordan, highly competitive and not wanting April to get ahead of him in the workbook, finally landed in his chair. The movement that he could not contain while sitting animated his small legs, which dangled three inches off the floor. (I always had a step under his chair for his feet to rest on, but his leg swinging always swooshed it away.) His legs swung wildly back and forth, matching

the prune-chewing motion of his mouth, their momentum caus-
ing the table to tremble as if in an earthquake.

"The table's moving, I'm scared," April said.

Jordan giggled and April slowly looked under the table, a look
of understanding spreading across her face. Another small light-
bulb lit up.

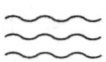

~~~~~

Two People at a Table

by Irene Sardanis

I didn't notice them at first. The couple. My dark depression over another heartbreak prevented me from seeing anybody when I entered the New York café. There went one more relationship in the garbage heap. Me, a 50-year-old washout with two divorces behind me, completely disillusioned at having a meaningful relationship with any guy. Surely I should have learned from my past mistakes. The good, submissive wife to domineering husbands. What's wrong with this picture? What's wrong with me?

After several months of on-line dating, I thought I'd had the routine down pat. Just answer the ads, go out and meet new men. And I did.

There was J, who worked in construction and loved hiking and nature. I was attracted. Good looks and bulging muscles on his arms. He seemed interested. Yet after a few coffee dates, he stopped calling. Just like that. Was it my perfume? Or that I wasn't athletic enough?

Then there was E, who loved salsa dancing. So did I. We'd go out to clubs, but salsa was all he loved. What he wanted was a dance partner, not a relationship.

There was M., the unemployed musician, who at the end of the evening of our first date pulled me close, kissed me and said he was crazy about me. So, could we move in together? Way too fast for me.

The latest one, T., an Engineer from Silicon Valley, that one broke my heart. When we first met I thought I'd won the lotto. We shared a love of good books, theater, film noir, and discussing them over gourmet dinners and wine. He wasn't tall, a bit over-weight, and not a sharp dresser, but he was intelligent, thoughtful, brought chocolate and flowers, embraced me warmly at the end of our dates. I should have suspected something was wrong when he never offered to meet at his place.

"It's more comfortable meeting you at cafés and your apart-ment," he said, touching my face. "My place is such a mess."

Hmm. Something didn't feel right. Was he married? Living with someone? "No," he said laughing. "I just like taking time to get to know one another."

I agreed to be patient. Why not? He was not like some of the oth-er guys who pounced on me after a first date. T. was different. He said he liked the way I dressed (casual) and said, "You're my pretty girl." So what if it was a line. I was falling for the guy.

We'd been dating for a few months and I pressed to see his messy apartment. Okay, I wanted to see if there was room for me in it and offered to cook dinner there. He declined.

Finally, he confessed. "This is hard to tell you, but the real reason we can't meet at my house is," and he looked down, embarrassed, "I live with my mother and she doesn't want me to bring any girl-friends to the place." When he brought someone over months be-fore, it didn't turn out well. "My mother threw her out."

What? Let's see. The guy was in his mid-50s, never been married. Why didn't I suspect something was wrong? Still, I pursued. We talked about it.

"Maybe she'll like me," I offered.

He wouldn't budge. I was good enough to date, but not good enough to meet his mother. Our relationship was like a fortress I couldn't penetrate. He also 'fessed up to not wanting to get serious with me. With great resistance to end it with "Mamma's Boy," I split. I stayed in bed for a week.

Nothing seemed to be working in my life in California. I needed a get-away to get some clarity. A writing conference in New York looked like a good escape. Maybe I'd meet someone exciting at the conference. Fat chance with my luck.

After settling into my New York hotel, I rushed to a corner café for breakfast before attending the seminar. The small dining room was crowded with everyone talking, grabbing their cup of coffee and a bagel. I ordered my latte and croissant.

I found an empty table in the back. I took a bite of my croissant and a sip of my coffee. Then I saw the couple at the next table.

He looked like a young Clint Eastwood. Gorgeous in a rugged way. He was about six feet tall, slender with broad shoulders, deep blue eyes. He wore a tan sports jacket and a black shirt. I imagined he was a model for some fashion magazine. The woman was also tall, blonde hair to her shoulders. She had on a coral blouse and tailored white slacks. The only jewelry she wore was gold hooped earrings and a plain gold bracelet. I pictured her as an art director, an interior decorator, someone artistic. Both looked to be in their thirties, and the way they looked at each other, oh, so much in love.

He watched the woman's face intently, touched her arm, holding it gently, his eyes transfixed on hers. He reached over, whispered something and kissed her cheek. I felt an inexplicable longing for a man like that.

It was obvious this couple was devoted to one another. They were oblivious to their surroundings. Their attention was on each other. Their coffee and toast sat between them, just like me, ignored. They didn't notice my stares. They just talked, touched, and laughed together.

A flood of yearning came up and tightened my throat; like yesterday's bad pizza it stuck there like a lump I couldn't swallow or throw up. *Gimme some of that*, I thought greedily. I ached for someone to look at me, lean over and kiss my cheek and smile just like that man with his lover.

Why was I attracted to the guys who were too shy to put their arms around my shoulder, kiss me, lie to me and tell me how beautiful I looked? I was ashamed to admit how sad and lonely I felt glued to their intimate interaction. Honestly, I wanted all of it, the look, the touch, the kiss with tender words of love.

I checked my watch. Sigh. Back to reality. Time to get going to the conference. I got up to leave and stopped at their table. "Excuse me," I said shyly, "but it has been so wonderful to watch you two. You are a beautiful couple and so in love. I'll bet you are newlyweds."

They both laughed. "No, we're actors," he said, amused. "We're not married. We're rehearsing for a play, 'Love Letters.' It's playing off Broadway on 49th Street. Come over and see us tonight," he said, shaking my hand. "I'm glad you enjoyed our performance."

Gasp. Groan. I turned and left quickly.

At the cash register I felt a tap on my shoulder. A familiar face. "Hey," a man's voice said from behind. I turned to see who it was. "You probably don't remember me," he said with a grin, "but weren't you the greeter last year at the writer's conference in L.A?" I recognized him, noticed his tall strong-featured looks and warm smile.

I took a risk. "Yes, that was me. So, are you in New York for the conference at the Waldorf?" I asked. "Yes I am," he said. "Okay if I walk over with you?"

I took his arm. "Definitely." I said. "Very definitely."

Homeless, Not Helpless

by Carol Gieg

My husband, Luis, and I were taking a walk in our neighborhood one day, when we spied something parked near our condominium complex. The large cart (maybe 4 x 2 feet) looked oddly out of place, sitting alone in a field of overgrown weeds just one block from Main Street.

It consisted of a plywood box with a bicycle wheel strapped on each side, serving as tires. A long piece of steel tubing stretched from one side to the other, fashioned to pull the contraption.

Curious, we walked over to take a closer look, then saw a sleeping bag spread out on the ground. A man lay inside, his face deeply lined and gray in pallor. The grizzled beard and hair at the temples were flecked with gray. He was sound asleep and oblivious to the world.

As we drew closer, he must have heard us, because suddenly, his eyes flew open. He recoiled in horror, then greeted us with, "Shit! Oh, shit!"

Frantically yanking himself out of the sleeping bag, he leapt up, fully dressed, minus the shoes. His jeans were tattered and frayed at the seams, his shirt so deeply stained that it was impossible to guess what the original colors might have been.

Never taking his eyes off us, he quickly rolled up the sleeping bag and tossed it into the cart, where it lay on top of the sum total of his worldly possessions.

These included a battered cooking pot and ladle, two McDonald's wrappers, a bicycle pump, a moth-eaten blanket, two large plastic bags and a large jug of water. Tucked neatly into one corner was a small pile of books, the uppermost one being a Bible.

"Just catching some shut eye," he frantically tried to explain.

"Please relax. We're not the police or anything," I reassured him.

My husband echoed this with, "Yeah, we just saw you and came over to ask if we could help."

The man said nothing more but turned and tried to pull the cart in the opposite direction.

Because of one flat tire, it wouldn't budge. Finally, surrendering to the effort, he paused and peered at us, still uncertain about our intentions.

"Name's Luis," my husband began, offering his hand, "and you?" He seemed a little startled, hesitated a moment, then answered, "Mark."

"That's some contraption ya' got there! Make it yourself?" Luis asked.

"Yep. Found the parts around here and there and nailed it all together. I needed something to haul my stuff around."

"How do you keep it supported from underneath?" Luis asked.

"Here, take a look," Mark said, squatting down beside the cart. Luis joined him to peer up at the steel rods crisscrossing under the wood.

"Oh, I see what you mean. Good idea!" said Luis.

My husband, having found a kindred spirit, continued talking with Mark about the virtues of certain materials being used for certain functions and how to come up with an overall plan for accomplishing their endeavors. Both of them were pretty handy regarding engineering projects of daily life. In fact, Mark was right in sync with Luis's pet peeve:

"Nobody knows how to do anything for themselves anymore!"

"Yeah, can't even change a lightbulb without asking for help, can they?" agreed Mark wholeheartedly.

During this one short conversation, Mark and Luis seemed to be finding more in common than not. They continued bantering on like this for a few more minutes. Then, Mark asked, "You guys live around here?"

"Yes," I answered, "about a half a mile down the street. We moved here six months ago from Santa Rosa."

"Oh, I had a brother who lived there once, but he moved back East where we're from."

"Don't you have any other family around?" I asked innocently.

He hesitated for a moment, apparently searching for just the right words.

"No, I'm from New York. Came out here a couple of years ago. I'm a construction worker and construction dried up back there, so I headed West. California was having a big building boom at that time."

He turned to my husband, "Sure not like that anymore, huh?"

"You got that right," Luis emphatically agreed.

Eventually, Mark asked, "So where were you two headed when you stopped by?"

"Just taking a walk over to church," I explained.

"I better get going too. It won't be long before the police tell me to. Also, a few days ago some kids were harassing me—you know, pointing, laughing at me, and imitating me snoring, after I woke up!"

He put out his hand to shake Luis's. "Nice talking to you both," with a nod toward me.

"Maybe I'll see you around sometime."

As we turned to leave, I asked him, "Anything we can do to help you? Maybe you could use a new sleeping bag or some food or maybe a new coat? Winter's right around the corner," I said.

"No thanks, I'm good," he replied.

He paused for a moment, thought better of it and added, "A

bicycle tire tube would help and, since you're headed to church, anyway, would you ask people to send a few prayers out for me?"

"Of course, Mark, of course," I said, struck by the fact that he hadn't asked for a handout, just some hope in a seemingly hopeless situation.

I glanced back as we walked away. He was wearing a smile on his face for the first time since we'd met him.

I waved, then turned to Luis, "You know, I think he enjoyed the conversation with us as much as we did with him. I mean, I bet he's always being either pitied or harassed, never really seen as anything but homeless."

"Yes," Luis agreed, "that cursed homelessness could happen to any of us."

We never did catch sight of him again, though we dropped a new bicycle tube in the place we'd seen him. We knew that he'd accommodated better than most anyone could, was a proud and strong man, despite his circumstances—well deserving of respect—homeless, but certainly not helpless.

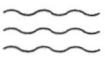

~~~~~~~

Whisper

by Stephen Schelling

Y ou said hello. I said hello. Before sitting, we hugged like friends do, warmly but not too tight. We talked. It felt awkward because the talk was small. I said words, but not the ones I hoped to say. You didn't say the words I hoped to hear.

We sat in a bar. Shiny and lacquered wood made up the inside—the bar counter, the tables, the chairs, and the walls, with many colors of brown in lines, whorls, and patterns. It looked smooth but felt sticky in many places. I didn't know the bar, but you did, because you lived in this town and I didn't. I was visiting, visiting others, not you, but you lived there, too. I wanted to see you.

Before you came, I sat at the bar alone, because my wife wasn't with me. She was at my father's home with my family. I had told her I was going out because I needed to go out, and that was the only explanation I had given her, and it was enough. But you, the woman I am talking to—we knew each other when we were younger—you are not alone. Your boyfriend is in another room of the bar with his friends. When I asked to meet, you said sure, that you knew this little bar nearby. You and your boyfriend could meet me that evening. I said sure, even though I wished it were only you who would meet me that evening.

We sat at the counter in the bar on stools that were not made of wood but of painted-black metal and were bolted into the floor at their bases. The black fake leather seats, variegated in faded grays and off-whites, were cracked in numerous places. We both ordered beer from the tap but different kinds and clinked the glasses softly and took a sip each before setting them back on the bare counter. There were no coasters, and none were needed in a place like this. Froth bubbled and danced with no apparent meaning or purpose inside both glasses after they clunked onto the wood.

Then, I told you I had loved you for a long time. You said you knew, like you had expected me to say that all along and had always known. I didn't ask if you had loved me too. You didn't say. That unknown was left between us. I went on to say if I had told you earlier, if we had ever been together, we wouldn't be here now. We wouldn't be friends. You said you knew, again. I smiled sadly. You smiled as if to say you were sorry.

We said little, dancing around saying anything of meaning or purpose. Finally, I got up and so did you, our drinks unfinished, barely even sipped, bubbles cascading into nothing. You walked past me but stopped and turned back. You were between me and the door to the outside world, a world where we existed separately. You looked up at me because I am tall and you are not. It was that way when we knew each other and still is. We stood there not speaking, only looking, my eyes regarding your eyes and your eyes regarding mine back. I remembered your eyes from back then, and now still the same color but, around them, you have grown older, just like the area around mine. I remembered your eyes always full of joy, and my eyes feeling joy when they looked into yours. Now, yours are doleful, like they have seen many sad things and know the pain of loss. Only the color remains the same.

You leaned toward me with your searching eyes. Your feet followed, shuffling in step. You reached forward with your face and kissed me, on the lips, a real kiss, a kiss that said what you had left unknown. Now I knew and will always know. I reached down with my face and kissed back, also a real kiss, a kiss that said what you already knew.

You leaned back. I leaned up. We smiled, the same smiles again, smiles that knew what happened was now past, and would always stay that way. Then you walked away out of sight into another room in the bar where I wasn't. I left too, through the door into a world where you weren't and would never be. I didn't know where I was going. It didn't matter.

Daddy Never Learned to Say "No"

by Carolyn Plath

*"Daddy Never Learned to Say 'No'" and "Jim Lyons and the Shotgun"
are excerpts from my memoir-in-progress, working title,* Glenn's Sister.
*It takes place in Oklahoma and spans the decades from the 1950s to
now. In these excerpts, readers will find references to facts revealed in
other chapters, including a time when my family lived in Abadan, Iran.
I was present for many of the events in the book. Often, details are
included from second-hand accounts that came to me from my brother,
Glenn, and from others who were there when I wasn't.*

After the divorce, my Daddy took me places. He'd never
done that before and so now I began to learn about him,
fit him into my puzzle of the world. Each new observation, every fresh experience, served to widen my view and formulate my assessment of the way things were in his world and how
things were for me, and Momma, and my brother Glenn.

Daddy took me to the practice range where he shot clay pigeons:
100 in a row, 150, 200 without a miss. He wore a vest with patches
on it proclaiming his prowess with a shotgun.

We drove out to Harvey Young Airport where he kept his plane, a Piper Cub J-3, a two-seater. I watched him while he tinkered with it and gave instructions to the mechanic, Manuel. Daddy called him "manual," like a book.

He flew me to air shows where we watched stunt planes do snap rolls and barrel rolls and hammerhead stalls. He knew some of the pilots. They talked about gs and ailerons while I leaned into his leg.

When we flew, I sat in the front seat of the Piper and he worked the stick from the tandem seat behind me. I still couldn't see over the dash except up at the sky—white with clouds, indecipherable. Once, on a trip back from Kansas, when it came time to switch to the reserve tank of gas as he'd instructed me to do, I turned the lever too far, past the notch he'd shown me, and soon, starved of fuel, the engine began to sputter. In an instant Daddy threw off his seatbelt, surged over my seat back and clicked the lever into its proper place. Replenished, the engine returned to its droning, we leveled out and flew toward home, our hearts racing.

My Daddy stood 6'6" tall. I had to skip and hop to keep up with his long stride. He always got attention, and I did too, when we were together. "You gotta run to keep up, huh, Little Lady?" a man might say when passing us on the sidewalk. At the 7-11, the cashier flirted with him by flattering me. "What a pretty little girl! Those blue, blue eyes!"

When this happened, I put my chin on my chest. No one taught me how to accept a compliment. But Daddy would smile. No one taught him how to say no.

Daddy's Corvette was a 1957 hard top convertible. He unlatched the hard top and we lifted it off the car and onto the front porch. It was heavy for me, but I could do it. Then we drove with the sun in our faces.

Daddy had aviator sunglasses, like James Bond. If we passed other Corvettes, he lifted two fingers off the steering wheel in acknowledgement. Other drivers gave us a wave in return.

The Corvette was a two-seater, no room for anyone else. Glenn didn't go. He didn't go to the practice range or the airport. I wondered, but never asked, why he wasn't included. We could have squeezed him in.

Very early one summer morning when I was nine, Daddy parked at the curb in front of our house with a suitcase and a foldout Texaco map of the USA. Mom had packed a bag for me. Daddy and I were going to California to see Grandma!

Daddy put my bag next to his in the Corvette's trunk and a pillow on the console. When I settled into my red leather bucket seat Daddy expanded the road map and stretched it across my lap. "Here we are," he said, pointing to Tulsa. "And here's Grandma," his big hand slid left as he dragged his finger west along Route 66 to Los Angeles. "Make sure we don't get lost!"

I could only smile.

He turned the key and the Corvette's throaty rumble said, "Excitement!" He revved the engine a couple of times and we waved at my mom on the porch, he with his left hand and a half-smile, head tilted down to see her; I with my right hand and roller-coaster grin. That must have been Glenn in the shadow behind her, the screen door obscuring his expression. He turned away when Daddy revved the engine again and eased off the clutch. We crawled away from the curb and accelerated down the block.

My brother Glenn was named for Daddy's best friend Glenn. We stopped at Big Glenn's house that morning. "Wait here," Daddy said and swiveled. He folded each long leg up to his chest, then out of the car. Big Glenn opened the screen door and smiled, his teeth too large and perfect, as Daddy strode up the walk. When they came out a few minutes later, Daddy had something wrapped in a faded blue towel under his arm.

"See you in a couple of weeks," Daddy said to Glenn, as he reversed the process of managing his legs to get back behind the wheel. Glenn leaned down and smiled at me. "Say 'hi' to your Grandma!"

"Okay," I said. The prospect thrilled me.

Daddy lifted the pillow and put the towel-wrapped object on the console underneath. The frayed edge of the towel fell open to reveal a handgun, a square looking one, an automatic.

"Don't you worry about that; it'll keep us safe," Daddy said. "Don't touch it either. It won't bother you under the pillow."

He gunned the Corvette's engine, and this time we leapt away from the curb, down the block, and onto the road toward the highway.

Turned sideways in my seat to nap as we drove, I rested my head on the pillow. I could feel it there, the gun. I didn't worry about it. I knew we were safe. Once, in my sleep, I pushed my hand under the pillow. When my fingers bumped the hard metal, I woke and sat up in one motion, looking at my dad, fearing he'd know I touched the gun. "Hey," he said with a rare smile. "Did you sleep?" I nodded.

"We're leaving Oklahoma."

I opened the map and he pointed to the Texas panhandle. Then he hunkered over the steering wheel and said, "Scratch my back?" I always obliged.

We pressed on through Amarillo toward Tucumcari, left the pale yellows of Texas and took on the ruddy reds of the New Mexico desert. Once we saw a coyote as he ambled away from the highway. He turned as he went and threw an accusatory glance over his bony shoulder. Dusk gathered as we climbed up through the Sandia Mountains. At the crest, Albuquerque stretched twinkling before us.

Daddy and I smiled at each other. I remember feeling pleased by this, and even then, I made a mental note of the occurrence—two smiles in one day. Daddy liked being on the road.

"It's been a long time since lunch," he said. "Let's find something to eat and a place to sleep tonight." I sat up tall and straightened my shirt.

Soon, we turned off the highway into the gravel lot of the Star Café. "Eat," its neon sign commanded. The Lobo Motel, "Gateway to the Sandia Crest," sat next door. We locked the Corvette and went toward the café lights. People turned when we appeared, the giant and the little girl. Daddy directed me to a booth, its green vinyl cold against my skinny legs.

Our waitress's nametag read "Darlene." She came to our booth immediately with menus in her armpit, utensils folded into paper napkins in one hand, and two plastic glasses filled with ice water in the other. Somehow, she sat it all on the corner of the table, handed us our menus, and pulled a damp cloth from her forearm. She leaned across the table and made sweeping motions with the cloth, wiping away nothing, her breasts hanging low.

Darlene's hair was mostly blonde and pretty stiff. Her bangs made a cylinder on her forehead. Her skin was smooth, her eyes clear brown with black liner and mascara, and her lips orange sherbet to match her uniform.

She smiled at my daddy and said, "You folks been on the road awhile?" I guess it showed.

Daddy smiled back, "Six this morning."

"Let me get you some coffee—or, will you stay the night?"

"We'll stay," he said.

"Then decaf it is," Darlene smiled again. "Would you like a Coke, sweetie?" I nodded yes and she turned away.

Daddy watched her go and I remembered a time before the divorce when he and Momma and Glenn and I were all in the Turnpike Cruiser after watching "Up Periscope!" at the Admiral Twin drive-in theater. Daddy drove us across the street to the A&W Root Beer stand. A girl there, a carhop, took our order for root beer floats and turned to go. Daddy watched her too.

"I want to be a carhop!" I chirped.

"Your butt's not big enough," Momma replied flatly.

Darlene returned with my Coke and Daddy's coffee, a sugar bowl, and a little metal pitcher full up with cream.

"What are you hungry for?"

Daddy ordered chicken fried steak, mashed potatoes, brown gravy, and green beans. I had a grilled cheese sandwich and French fries. We ate in silence. I sucked my shiny fingers between each bite.

"How 'bout some pie?"

Daddy looked up to see Darlene cock her hip and tilt her head. "We've got apple, cherry, pecan, coconut cream, and lemon meringue." No question. We would have lemon meringue.

Our wide slices of yellow custard arrived with stiff white meringue two inches tall. Darlene gave us fresh forks and we dug in. She lingered near the booth for a moment. "Good, huh?" We both nodded and smiled.

She moved to the booth next to ours, leaned over it and wiped more nothing from the table there. "So . . . you're headed out in the morning?" she ventured.

Daddy didn't answer right away. He watched her while he finished a bite of crust. He seemed to measure her and his response.

"Yeah, I hope I'll be able to sleep tonight."

She smiled and turned toward the cash register. Daddy watched again for a moment then smiled to himself as he returned to the sweet tang of lemon custard.

We checked into the Lobo Motel and Daddy moved the Corvette in front of Room #3 facing the gravel lot. Twin beds and a TV on a stand. The rabbit ears had aluminum foil crumpled onto them. Daddy sat on the end of his bed and took off his enormous shoes. He set them aside and curled his back like he did in the car when he wanted me to scratch it.

"Get into your pjs and get in the bed." I hoped we could turn on the TV, but I wouldn't ask. We would watch TV if Daddy wanted to. I took my toothbrush into the tiny bathroom and changed.

When I came out, Daddy was stooped over the TV turning the dial from channel 3 to 4 to 6. He wiggled the antenna at each new setting with no appreciable effect. A snowy picture showed an Albuquerque newsman reading his script. Different channel, different newsman.

I got under the stiff white sheets and propped the scratchy pillow behind my neck. Daddy stretched out onto his bed; his feet extended past the foot of it. He wrestled his pillow a bit too and focused on the newsman. The volume low; the newsman's report monotone, like Daddy's voice. He stared at the screen. There would be no conversation and soon I fell fast asleep.

A click and another click woke me. The room was dark except for the fluttering glow of the test pattern on the TV screen, a black-and-white segmented target with a line drawing in the center of an Indian chief in profile. Just then the door opened, and in the widening rectangle of light from the Lobo Motel's exterior, Daddy's lanky silhouette emerged. He was coming in.

I shut my eyes and pretended to sleep. He closed the door without a sound and turned toward the room. He sat on the end of his bed again and turned the TV off. He undressed in the dark and got under the covers in his underwear. Soon his breathing became slow and regular.

He woke me the next morning with a shake of my shoulder. He was already dressed. "Let's go," he said. I knew to get up right away and get started no matter how groggy I felt.

We stepped out of Room #3 into a cool and damp first light. Two red pick-up trucks and a tan VW camper angled toward the windows of the Star Café. Fluorescence glowed from inside brighter than the fledgling dawn around us.

We crunched across the gravel of the parking lot into the café, and sat at the counter this time, reflecting our need to get back on the road. Sharon, a squat waitress in the familiar orange-sherbet uniform, brought water, a ceramic coffee mug, and menus. I looked around for Darlene.

Daddy saw me looking and seemed to understand my unspoken question.

"She works nights," he said.

~~~~~~~

Jim Lyons and the Shotgun

by Carolyn Plath

It took years for me to piece together the parallel worlds of my parents. When my dad drove away from the house with his work shirts in the Corvette and tears in his eyes, I, like a dull-witted neighbor, had an ill-formed thought about an argument between them that kept me up one night. An amorphous question floated at the periphery, low to the ground like smoke from a dwindling campfire beyond the range of my comprehension.

I remember Mom told me once that the best place to hide things from Daddy was in her Kotex box. "He will never look in there," she said. A silverfish of confusion slipped to the seam of my consciousness—What would she be hiding from Daddy? Why must she hide things from him?—and wriggled itself away into the file marked "Reopen When It's Too Late to Ask." "Do Not Open Until Your Own Marriage is Falling Apart and Everyone Who Knows Anything About This Kind of Stuff is Dead." Yeah, good idea, keep it there.

When my Daddy stared at that carhop's ass, or picked up a woman from the corner once when I was staying the weekend with him, those stray scraps of information went into the shoebox of my ill-equipped mind, only to produce wonder or forehead slaps later, much later.

Maybe Mom dated after she and Daddy split. Maybe she was even open about it, but I don't think so. I only knew she went to work teaching math at Nathan Hale High School on the other side of town. Glenn and I went to school close to the house and had the place to ourselves in the afternoons before she could get home from her school to supervise. We lived our lives, she lived hers; I guess Daddy lived his life too.

But Jim Lyons's arrival mandated adjustments across all fronts.

Jim taught shop at my mom's school. No doubt they met there. But the appeal? The attraction? I still don't get it. I don't remember seeing them courting, or any breaking-in period. I don't remember Mom introducing us, though surely she did. All I know for certain is they got married. He moved in with us. It didn't go well.

I was gangly and hesitant then. Thirteen years old. Compliant. I wanted everyone to be happy and to like me. That's how it was with Jim. I had questions about him—"Where did he come from?" or, "What's he doing here?"—but they remained formless, like Jim himself—vague; non-committal. And Mom seemed energized, happy. So I never asked. Mostly I wanted peace in the house.

I had been flustered when kids at school asked why my mom's last name was different from mine. I felt confused, embarrassed for not knowing. I didn't know why Jim was there or how to explain anything. An enormous flood of relief washed through me when one day after school I happened to be standing near Becky McNamara, THE cutest, most popular girl in the seventh grade, and someone asked her why her mom's name was different from hers. Becky shrugged and said casually, "She got remarried."

That's it! That's what I'll say! Hallelujah! My mom got remarried!

Glenn, on the other hand, was suspicious of Jim from the start. But, his interactions with Jim were neither dismissive nor open, rather, ostensibly neutral. Glenn observed this new arrival as a scientist would, holding in reserve his assessment of a specimen in a petri dish.

That changed the instant Jim called Glenn an oddball.

They were looking at a group picture of the two of us and all our cousins. It must have been taken at Easter a couple of years before. All eleven of us were lined up in Grandma's front yard, squinting into the sun. The other boys wore Wrangler's jeans and buzz-cut hair. Jesse's boys looked like the 4-H kids they were, muscular, tan. Teetum's boys were awkward, smiling goofy smiles, T-shirts askew. And Glenn, already tuned into the British invasion, looked it, with his over-the-ears, mop-cut hair brushed forward, long-sleeved white shirt with over-sized pointed collars and a paisley brocade vest.

"You just don't fit in, buddy," Jim tapped Glenn's face in the snapshot and chuckled in the deliberate, cynical manner we'd already come to expect. He adjusted his posture, sitting taller, gleeful to point out the difference. Of all the things to quip about, he'd stumbled on the one that pierced Glenn's confidence—his uncertainty about belonging in the family. Glenn pulled away, flushed with anger and said, "Fuck you."

He stood to leave and Jim laughed again and called after him, "It's just a joke. What're you so mad about?" Jim turned to look at Mom with feigned innocence. "What did I do?"

After that, Glenn didn't care about neutrality or peace. He made no effort to disguise his distaste for our new step-dad.

Jim was more guarded, too. He didn't make any more overt comments about Glenn, and his eyes always followed Glenn in the room. He might have to tilt the top edge of the newspaper down to see Glenn move from the hallway across the corner of the living room, through the dining room, and into the kitchen.

Always wary. Glenn made no eye contact. Why would he look at a worm on the sidewalk?

Meals became strategic undertakings with timing, placement, and word choice tactical imperatives. If Jim spoke, let's say at dinnertime, to voice how he preferred his hamburger, Glenn would snort at his choice. And whatever Jim's choice was, Glenn would choose the opposite.

Jim did not try to raise us, or to participate in our lives. He seemed an observer, a bemused critic. He might comment on my new school clothes, but never on Glenn's comings and goings. The last time he asked Glenn where he was going, Glenn said he was going to get drunk and fuck a sheep.

By contrast, Jim seemed to find me diverting. Each summer I put my visionary nature and organizational skills to work casting neighborhood kids in talent shows. Once, under my direction, half a dozen of us performed "Blue Hawaii" in the living room for Mom and Jim. I taped a penny to the arm of the hi-fi and carefully dropped the needle on the space leading to the correct band of Elvis's album. My friends and I sang along: "Night and you, and blue Hawa-a-a-ii." We did an awkward hula and swayed our arms side-to-side, imagining ocean breezes and a twinkle in the eye of The King. Jim laughed and clapped asking, "Who did the choreography?" I felt unsure since I didn't know the word. But Mom looked happy too, and nodded, so I said, "I did."

More than once Jim hurt my mom's feelings. I remember a night when she was changing clothes and changing clothes, getting ready to go back to school for a PTA meeting. Jim and I were at the kitchen table, he with the ever-present newspaper; I picked at a pork chop.

Mom came in wearing her third outfit, a skirt and sweater. She had gained weight and the skirt was tight. "How's this?" she asked, holding her breath, shoulders up, miserable with rounded belly and rounded butt.

"Is your skirt supposed to cup under like that?" Jim said with his hand forming said cup and scooping to show what he saw.

Mom sputtered and tears came to her eyes. She tugged at the sweater as she rushed from the room grazing the doorjamb as she went. Jim went back to his newspaper, and I could hear mom thrashing about in her bedroom. She left out the other door, through the living room, closing the front door firmly and letting the screen door slam.

I kept my head down as she started her '57 Mercury Turnpike

Cruiser—the one my dad bought her after we came home from Abadan—and backed out of the driveway. When she pulled away from the house, Jim folded the newspaper and carried it with him to the living room and sat down. The TV still didn't work. Even with him there we couldn't afford to get it fixed. He re-opened the paper and started over.

They argued when she came home that night, Mom and Jim. I could hear their voices, his measured and infuriating. Mom's clipped and sarcastic. Glenn probably heard them too; his room was just across the hall.

By now Glenn was sixteen and plenty angry. He stayed gone most of the time. I remember a time when he came through the house to get something from his room, Jim said, "Well! Look who dropped by! Look what the cat dragged in!"

Glenn, walking swiftly, barely turned his head as he lifted the middle finger of his left hand. Moments later, he came back through the room in the opposite direction with his pale yellow windbreaker over his arm. This time, he showed the middle finger of his right hand. Jim sniffed and shook his head, chuckling to himself.

Outside, Glenn jumped into the passenger seat of his best friend Doug's Oldsmobile. I could only hear the last word in his sentence when they lurched backwards out the driveway—"asshole." Dropping the Olds into drive, Doug managed to squeal the tires. The big sedan sank low in back and rose in front as they roared down 112th East Avenue, each boy with an elbow on his respective window frame.

By now, Jim had been in the house two years. He taught woodshop and came home at 4:15 every afternoon in a short-sleeved plaid shirt and Lee jeans. No lesson plans, no papers to grade. He settled in the same corner of the couch where my Daddy used to sit and waited for my mom and dinner.

Before he moved in, the toilet seat in our bathroom wobbled and slipped to the side when you sat. It still did. The frame of the window over the kitchen sink rotted after years of north wind and rain. Now the wind whistled through the porous corner of the wood, and the spongy wood stayed in place if you forced the glass upward to let in a breeze. The door from the kitchen into the garage hung askew on hinges with stripped screws. We developed a technique of "lift and close" to get it back in place if we opened it. And the screen to the back door leaned against the side of the house before Jim Lyons appeared. It also failed to catch the wood-shop teacher's attention.

I don't know if Jim gave my mom any money. I do know we didn't eat any better after he moved in. Maybe more regularly. He had his expectations for meals by the clock.

They began to argue. Mom told me years later, after we learned Jim died of a brain tumor, that he had changed suddenly during their short marriage. His personality changed, she said. According to her, he went from good guy to bad guy in pretty short order. She thought the tumor explained it. I had no recollection of the good guy.

Glenn wouldn't have described a change in Jim. He saw Jim as an interloper, a pretender, an offending detractor with an arrogant smirk.

Each taunted the other. Glenn, with the unreasonable certainty only a teenager can muster. Jim, with the foolish arrogance of a poker player drawing on an inside straight. They picked at each other, each taking delight in the acrimonious game.

Of a morning, we could find Jim at the kitchen table in his jeans and plaid shirt, his thinning hair brushed straight back from his face. It had receded on the sides of his forehead leaving a strip down the center of longer strands Brylcreemed into stasis. His forearm rested next to his cereal bowl, spoon poised for the next scoop. He waited Glenn out, smiling to himself when Glenn paced into the room. When Glenn chose not to eat rather than share the space, Jim counted that as a victory.

Glenn spit on the windshield of Jim's truck every morning when he left for school, savoring the effort and the effect. It pleased him most when a gooey glob landed just at driver's eye level.

Day after day, the struggle went on. Momma seemed to understand Glenn's point of view, but didn't try to intervene or explain one to the other. After all, Jim hadn't risen to the pre-game hype. Maybe she rationalized that things would smooth over, or that Glenn would move out soon enough. Maybe she just didn't know what to do.

But Glenn was formulating an idea.

On a Sunday afternoon Mom and I went to Skiatook to visit her best friend Sammye. While we were gone, Glenn said he emerged from a long sleep and headed for the kitchen. Jim was there ahead of him, standing and staring into our dingy, round-shouldered fridge. He leaned over and pushed aside the baloney in hopes of finding some of last night's meatloaf. He glanced to the side to find Glenn there, in line for something to eat.

He turned back to the fridge and began to whistle as he elongated his search. Maybe he'd need some grape jelly. No. What's this in the aluminum foil? Oh, it's that goulash with the crusty edge. Nope.

"Make up your mind and get out of my way," Glenn said.

Jim straightened up in the wedge of space made by the open door of the fridge. He smiled that infuriating smile and flinched at Glenn, a full body surge, making Glenn step back.

"I'll kill you, you stupid son of a bitch," Glenn said, as he turned away and headed back to his bedroom.

Jim laughed a little laugh, put a bowl of potato salad under his left arm and rested the baloney on the Saran Wrap stretched across the top. He balanced the mustard there, grabbed a head of iceberg lettuce, and swiveled toward the table; he bent his knee and shut the refrigerator door with his upturned heel.

I don't remember if Glenn said where he got the gun. Maybe it had been Grandpa's. I didn't know he had it—a shotgun with two long barrels side-by-side. It must have been in his closet or under his bed a long time. It was old looking and heavy. He was unaccustomed to wielding it. He said he paused outside his bedroom door and swung it awkwardly up to his shoulder.

He walked down the hall and crossed the living room with the gun swaying. When he rounded the corner in the dining room and when Jim came into view, he stopped and stabilized himself, spread his feet, put his cheek on the cool dry wood of the gun's stock and his finger on the trigger.

Jim sat as usual, back curved over his food, baloney, white bread, and yellow mustard. The potato salad sat with its weepy Saran Wrap skin peeled back. Jim held it hostage, his fork hovering.

He felt Glenn's presence more than he saw anything from his peripheral view. But he sat chewing like a cow, looking ahead, across the kitchen at...what? Crumbs on the countertops? Yesterday's breakfast dishes with egg yolks hardening? That north window he could have repaired? Rude and defiant, he took another bite of his sandwich and poked at the potato salad with his fork.

Glenn stood still and took shallow breaths, not noticing the weight of the gun now. No hurry.

Jim snorted and smiled to himself, and turned at last to see Glenn and the gun leveled at him.

His smirk fell and his features went round and wide; eyes, mouth, and nostrils now circles in stretched white skin. He wanted to say something, but no words came. He dropped the fork and pushed his chair back with the calves of his legs as he rose. The chair teetered and tipped backwards, its back bumped against the wall.

"Good," Glenn said. "Get up and go, you prick."

Jim moved his butt across the edge of the table, not wanting to get any closer to Glenn or to lose sight of him. He took a side step toward the door that led from the kitchen through the laundry room and into our mom's bedroom.

Glenn took two steps forward, kept his cheek on the smooth wood; his left eye squinted, his right eye followed Jim through the gun's metal notch of a sight at the end of the double barrels.

"Wait," Jim said. Afraid to turn his head, he bumbled and felt his way out of the room.

"No," Glenn said. "No more waiting. You gotta go, you fucking prick piece of shit."

Jim broke for the door, crashed through it, and slammed the door to the bedroom behind him.

Glenn stepped quickly. Never intending to open the door, he smashed the gun against it again and again for maximum clatter.

"Hurry up asshole!"

Jim flew across the bedroom, through the other door and into the hallway, out the front door and into his truck. Glenn leapt through the house, stepped onto the front porch and again brought the gun to his shoulder. He aimed it at the truck's windshield and smiled at the dried spot of spit he'd left there the night before.

Jim cranked up the truck, threw it into reverse, lurched backwards across the yard and over the curb onto 112th East Avenue. Glenn took two steps forward. Jim wrestled the truck into first gear, popped the clutch, and looking back over his shoulder, raced to the end of the block.

Glenn allowed the gun's barrel to drop and stood there in the sun for a good long while. He enjoyed deep breaths and thought of nothing in particular. Then he went in, sat on the couch, and waited for Mom and me to come home.

I don't remember seeing Jim after that, though he surely returned to gather his belongings. He and my mom divorced without incident; after all, there was little investment on either side. I looked for an effect on Mom, but none was perceptible. If she cried, or they hashed things out over the phone, I never knew. It was almost a non-event. The lost chapter of my mom's second husband. That stone created few ripples in this pond.

Like my Daddy, Jim was wrapped up, taped into a box, and gone.

The three of us, Mom, Glenn, and I, reverted to our routines. We only talked about Jim that one time when we came home and Glenn told us the story. Mom only said, "Oh," and "Oh," again. She didn't evince surprise or anger. She didn't wonder—not aloud anyway—where Jim went or if he would come back. Maybe she was in shock. Maybe she was relieved. If she'd been trying to figure out how to undo what she'd done by marrying Jim, that riddle had been solved with Glenn's direct approach.

Indeed, only Glenn seemed clear, as though he'd had a plan, carried it out, and anticipated the outcome. "Here," he said and showed us the rusty gun with its bent hammer. It wasn't loaded, and couldn't have fired if it had been.

That was a good thing.

Crossroads

Adriana

by Nicky Ruxton

They both stumbled when her high heel snagged the ivory lace trim at the bottom of her white satin gown. Like drunken monkeys, they tumbled into an open elevator and fell to the marble floor. His instinct was to protect the flutes and champagne bottle he'd pilfered from the reception, but the glasses slipped from his hand. Adriana, barefoot, wobbled herself upright. One high heel kicked off inside the elevator and the other white crystal beaded shoe rolled unnoticed into the hallway.

The elevator door snatched a swath of bridal fabric and chewed a section of beaded hem. Her Lancelot yanked the trapped fabric from the closed door and freed his intoxicated Guinevere. A ruined wedding dress was just one casualty of their unbridled passion.

Adriana was so inebriated she might have fallen down again, but Giovanni held her by the waist and propped her limp body against the mirrored wall. With the flutes forgotten, he lifted the cumbersome magnum by its neck up to his eager mouth and guzzled with greed. Adriana serenaded her sexy knight off key, yet no music accompanied their elevator rendezvous.

Giovanni drenched her lips with champagne and sloppy kisses. He smeared her mouth open with unrestrained desire. She was too delirious to care that he tasted of stale cigarettes. After the fuel of more alcohol, he declared, "Here's to the best man."

Her laughter was loose and giddy as he pushed his way into the perfume of her neck, then thrust a hand underneath layers of silk and taffeta. The ripped, beaded hemline wound around their feet like seaweed.

Neither one noticed that the elevator hadn't moved.

He was irresistible: his dimples, his Italian accent, his naughty boy charisma. Adriana was not in love with him, but exhilarated by his lavish attention. With his eyes on her from across a room, she sensed his heat. After sharing covert thrills in cars, hallways, and bathrooms, she hungered for their clandestine encounters.

She met him after she and Eric had begun to date. Giovanni and Eric were inseparable best friends with opposite tastes. Seductive Giovanni loved motocross, reggae concerts, and tequila. Practical Eric listened to classical music, drank an occasional beer, and was taken with environmental issues. Eric was a stable provider, Giovanni a matador.

His shirt half unbuttoned, her dress rumpled over rosy-patched flesh, spoke of their selfish urgency. A single satin shoe in the elevator's corner lay like a beached fish among flutes and loose crystal beads.

She was under her daredevil's spell. In a clumsy maneuver he pushed her pliant body onto the marble and groped beneath the beaded bodice. Unaware of their surroundings, drenched in spilled champagne, they tangled in lust on this, her wedding day.

Oblivious until the elevator door slid open, both passengers startled and stared up from their compromised position.

The father of the groom, Eric's proud tuxedoed dad, stood in the hallway with his wife. The color drained from her face as she gasped, clutching a silk purse in one hand and, in the other, a white beaded shoe.

~~~~~

Rail Rats

by Nicky Ruxton

Part I
Echo

I was on the short side of twenty-one, itching to slide into clubs, bars, and "twenty-one and over" pool halls that all wanted to keep me out for being a minor. See, I grew up in family billiard clubs, playing pool most days after school with my older brother, PJ, who was thirteen back then, and I was maybe nine. He showed me the ropes and how to make what he called "sure thang" bets.

Gambling was his vice and gambling's what took him down, but that's a whole 'nother story. PJ used to take me way across town to Moe's, where they ran coin-operated tables, you know, where ya slip quarters in the slots for timed play.

On school days PJ would bet on the down low on stupid kid shit, like how many kids in class had blue backpacks. Then, on the weekends, we'd play pool down at Moe's with his winnings. PJ was a troublemaker, taught me how to drink beer and smoke cigarettes. They called pool kids like us barn rats, or baby rats, cuz we was always underfoot and in the way. But, hey, that was ten years ago.

Finnegan's Place had the usual dive bar vibe with the stink of stale beer greeting ya at the front door. Walking inside, the sticky floor pulled at the bottom of my boots. The air back by the toilets smelled thick of piss and weed. I carried a fake ID, a pack of KOOLs, and a vial of blow in my leather jacket pocket, like a good Boy Scout—I believed in being prepared.

Sometimes I'd see college boys in the john snorting up fat lines to impress each other, but me, I did coke bumps inside a stall after I became a regular, after weighing the risks of getting caught. Funny, old man Finn wouldn't sell a lick of beer to a minor, but his bar's toilets smelled like a dispensary.

Kids partied outside in the parking lot before they slid into Finn's, which made easy pickings for me by the time they stumbled in. They drank too much, too fast, and were way too eager to show off for their friends. A lot of them punks were just looking for something to do, looking for a little action to brag about come Monday.

Man, when I was a teenager, I wasn't like that. I started winning pool money on the regular, so yeah, easy pickings at clubs, and it was good money. I kept my wits about me doing the cat/mouse thing PJ taught me. Sure, he had questionable integrity that rubbed off on me, but I had a back-pocket plan that he lacked, or gambled away.

My first time at Finnegan's a big guy wearing a short twisted 'fro sat alone at the bar counter, like a solitary crow. Dude didn't blink when I sat down next to him, even though I could have, maybe should have, kept an empty seat between us. A stubby glass of amber liquid stared up at him from the counter top. The drink's ice cubes reflected a yellow light bouncing off the bottles from behind the bar.

"What kind of whiskey ya drinking?" I asked.

"What kind of whiskey? What the fuck, you hitting on me?" he spit back.

"What, wait? Hey man, just making conversation."

"Just making conversation? Your mama teach you how to do

that, little girlie man?"

My body tensed and I slid off the barstool for a hasty retreat when he grabbed the arm of my leather jacket. Pulling me tight to his chest, my ear crushed against the side of his face.

"You a fag lover, Whitey?"

"Whoa! What the hell, Dude?" Ripping free from his grasp, I jumped back with my hands up in surrender. "I don't know what your deal is man, but I don't want any trouble, okay?"

He broke into spasms of laughter that threw me off guard.

"I don't want any trouble, okay?" he said, imitating me. "Settle down, little fucker, I'm just messing with you! Can't be too careful. Now come on and sit down, let me buy you a drink."

My heart raced faster than my mind could unscramble my thoughts. I wanted a drink and reached for my ID, but remembered my no-drink policy in first-time places. I heard PJ's voice in my head, "Keep your wits about you, you little turd, you gotta be able to read the room and focus on the hustle." My mouth opened, and "Coke" was all I said.

The big guy in a tight black shirt called to the bartender, "Hit me again and bring a Coke for my mop-headed friend here." He looked right at me and grinned. "Name's Charles Michael Eric Thomas, but everyone calls me Echo."

"You got four first names?" I managed to say. "What was your mama thinking?"

"My mama was a mean-ass drunk with a jail-sized meth habit, so, you know, I guess thinking wasn't exactly her forte."

Jesus, I didn't know if this guy was punking me, or what, but my fear relaxed. I related to something about him, but still I sat on the far edge of my seat just in case.

"So what'd they call you, bean pole?" He was goading me again.

"In school it was Little Sticks or Blue Fingers, but just Stix now."

"Well, Just Stix Now," he grinned a toothy smile, "in a few minutes your new pal Echo here is going to kick your ass with some fancy One-Pocket action."

Not sure how he knew I was itching to play. Never asked, never said. We talked for a while and I kept my soon-to-be-kicked ass flat on the barstool. Echo was pretty fucking funny. Told me he lived nearby, and that would be convenient later on. Swallowing his drink, he stretched his limbs to standing. Dude had to be over six three. Weighed like, I dunno, two twenty, two thirty with dope biceps that could crush me.

For sure he worked out. I considered sheet-rocker (but his mahogany hands looked too smooth for that), gym steroid user, or maybe he did a stint at San Quentin, but I didn't see any neck tats. I followed behind him to a nearby Brunswick table, a mere dingy in the wake of his mighty size.

Part II
Tournament Talk

I had an 18-ounce Canadian maple shaft, a *Viper Desperado*. Hell of a stick. Its leather wrap dampened long play vibrations and it had a built-in removable scuffer, to toughen up the tip. That detail came in handy when sizing up players with more ego than skill.

The *Viper* gave a subtle message in unfamiliar clubs. Forty and under pool geeks loved the engraved skull graphics, the scroll artwork on the butt and forearm. The old dogs, nah, they weren't impressed at all. It was strictly a bad-boy's calling card.

Most nights Echo and me hung out at either Finn's or Vic's Pub & Pool, both establishments nestled in the scrappy *Phat Patch* neighborhood where I lived. My apartment was in a crap part of San Francisco, but it was within walking distance to three bars. The two already mentioned had decent billiard set-ups, and the third, "Her Alibi," was good for $20 a game mid-week. It was a scene on the weekends, too many cougars trying to get laid and willing to pay.

It was a Tuesday night in June. Me and the big guy were pretty buzzed at Vic's, messing around racking and breaking, when Echo pointed to a poster thumbtacked to the wall.

"Yo, Stix, check this shit out." He tapped a finger against the poster.

"Gotta take a leak, Dude!"

"Hold the leak, Dude. This here's about a Pro Tournament, says any challenger can stake a table in the showcase. September, Atlantic City, four hundred bucks."

"O.K. Back in a sec. Grab me another beer, would you?'

"Beer ain't on the house, man," he yelled as I turned away.

"Fuck you!" I laughed and bounced off to the toilet, patting the vial inside my pocket.

The Atlantic City thing started out as a joke. Two rail rats sharing a dream, but the more we talked about it, we figured how to pull it off. When Echo told me Salvatore Reymundo, the best One-Pocket pool player in the world, was favored to win, well, it didn't take much convincing to start strategizing on the serious.

We decided to turn the Atlantic City trip into a poor man's working vacation, which described me pretty well. Echo had a decent enough temp job, but I was, you know, between gigs, if you didn't count hustling pool. After the tournament weekend we planned to pool our way down the coast to Florida for fun and traveling dough.

Hell, I was pumped. Echo was a good planner, sharp thinker, and me, I kept my eye on the prize, on the details that would fill our pockets with lots of green.

Part III
Prior to Atlantic City

In order for Echo and me to finance our cross-country trip, we needed an immediate plan for making some serious Benjamins. Agreeing to run a shortstop hustle outside San Francisco, Echo suggested a drive down to Santa Cruz, then head over to Santa Barbara. He said we could shake out lots of coin there. I got the impression maybe he lived there once, or went to school there. Dunno. Then we'd head to Oxnard and down through Encinitas where emptying wallets should be baby candy. He agreed it was

best to avoid LA where new sharks practiced, like stand-up come-
dians, to hone their skills and take your money. I was down for
whatever. I liked roading.

Could take maybe three, four, six weeks, so we kept revising our
plans. If we played strong and didn't get scratched for stealing, we
could go home up the five and wrangle a few inland towns along
the way. PJ would say, "don't stay long enough to let them fuckers
count your hairs."

Locals were wary of outsiders, but they did have the advantage
of knowing their rooms and table quirks, like which tables had
fast cloth or slopped. But rats are rats! Big Echo and me made an
unlikely looking twosome, so we could dial down on stealth mode
and manipulate most situations to our advantage. I said, "That's
our superpower, we're like bad ass Ninjas."

Mr. Charles Michael Eric Thomas said first things first; we needed to reserve a rental car for our West Coast shortstop. My car was
a piece of shit, and he relied on public transportation. Two people came to mind that might lend us something for a few weeks.
Possible to borrow Finn's old Chevy, but we'd have to replace the
dead alternator first, which was cheaper than a rental. I said I
could fix it, but I wasn't so sure.

Also, we had to spot our travel expense and pay Atlantic City
tournament fees up front. Echo was good at managing money, for
sure better than me. I tried to pay my bills and rent on time. I
didn't like borrowing or owing people, but gettin' a quality high
ate through a lot of dough. When asked, I just said I liked the snow
and had an expensive skiing habit. Living in proximity to Tahoe
nobody blinked twice.

Pressing the phone to my ear, I tried to sound casual when she
answered.

"Hey, Lena." I said, kinda holding my breath.

"Hey yourself, Shane. What'd you want?"

"Can't I call my sister without an agenda?"

"Not after eleven. I'm going to bed, what'd ya want?" She knew
I hated asking for favors, but what else could I do? My unease was

in the asking.

"Me and Echo are heading out for awhile, okay to drop the dog over?" I held my breath even though Lena always said yes. She loved me, and my monster dog, too.

"Jesus, Shane, it's always something with you. Aren't you going to ask me to spot you some cash too? Maybe lend you the car again?"

I wasn't sure if that was an invitation.

Six years older than me, I leaned on her when necessary. She had her own family, all stable and shit, little house in Brisbane, nice yard for kids and animals. Her husband didn't hate me, so that was a big plus, but he saw right through me from day one.

"Chill, Lena, I just need you to watch my beast for a few weeks. You know the kids love him, and if you could spring for fifty bucks, I'll pay you back with interest, swear to God."

She snickered away the tension between us. "Let's just leave God out of this!"

Part IV
Mambo

It was the day before the big money Pro Tournaments in Atlantic City began and headliners, like Salvatore Reymundo, showcased their skills for entertainment and side money. At four hundred bucks a pop, Sal-Rey could pick off six-to-eight players an hour shooting One-Pocket. A two-hour exhibition match might net him a cool 5K. Maybe he'd stay twice as long playing hopefuls, taking baby candy and dancing the Mambo all the way to the bank.

On Thursday's showcase player sheet, I was number five. A mixture of anticipation and nerves pretty much stole my cool. I sidled up as close to the rail as I could get to watch the first challenger. Echo was off getting coffees. "Too early for beer," he said, but I'd already hit a bump back at the motel.

Sal-Rey stretched his torso across the felt. Tension in his muscles clenched and released, adjusting his center point to stabilize his stance. Straddled between tabletop and toes, he inched forward, relaxing both shoulders. Those second-nature adjustments, almost imperceptible, spoke to those of us who studied his unorthodox techniques developed over a three-decade rise to the top.

From my position at the rail I saw his eyes narrow with laser focus past the cue line. His broad nose flared and his top lip curled just a bit. With an effortless touch he teased the last ball into his pocket. *Whoosh!* Claps rose as the tangerine five-ball rolled out of sight.

Shaking his hips for the crowd, he turned to the challenger who just lost and nodded in a show of respect. He gave the guy a playful slap on the back, and then posed for a few photos as the next wannabe chalked up. With each new player I imagined the ka-ching of four hundred dollars dropping into Mambo's pocket after a few minutes of play. Talented bastard!

Straining to see the next challenger racking up, I spilled the coffee Echo brought me down the front of my shirt. Yeah, I was nervous.

When it was my turn, I approached the table unable to breathe, my lungs locked up tight. I heard the crack and swoosh of my break scattering over the felt, then the dropping of Sal-Rey's balls down the rabbit hole one after another.

I focused hard on each minute of play, all nine of them, while my arms, you know, hung like phantom limbs twitching for their turn. Holding my *Viper* cue, I stood alert, eager to show him a hint of *my* talent, but yeah, that moment didn't come. It was "eight and out," as they say in One-Pocket, but I got nine glorious minutes stashed in my head forever.

Listen, it's not that I was cocky enough to think I could tournament play him, but the possibility got me off. Running balls with him was a dream, like a dying kid's last wish fulfilled, except I wasn't a kid or dying, so maybe it felt a little less great than that.

Next thing I remember, Echo tackled me from behind. "Come on, you cry baby loser," he laughed, "let's go get fucked up!"

A Dark Night at Moonridge Camp

by Judea Cavoto

The thing she didn't know was that life could be beautiful, a long flowing dream of being okay in her skin. She didn't know that there was a joy deep in the center of her that could dispel all the worries that followed her like stubborn rain-clouds. It could make her forget how small she became when her father walked out, weeks before her ninth birthday. And how lost she felt most of the time, in the sandstorm of her mother's needs and regrets.

Samantha didn't know any of this until the summer of 1998, when she was 12, and had been sent to her first sleep-away camp, which sat alongside the calmest, most forgiving lake she'd ever seen. Not a circular, blue man-made lake with dump-truck sandy beaches, but a real honest-to-goodness shining lake, whose waters shifted their moody colors of eucalyptus greens and crinkling browns quicker than her eyes could catch. Nor could she trace all the rough and wild edges of the grainy, mud-filled shores.

When she looked at the lake, her heart opened like a song that was thrilling and resonant in her chest—maybe a song by one of those classical guys from her dad's record collection. One of those composers was deaf, and her father had put a statue of this man's head in the living room. The statue had hair that swept back madly like he was driving in a convertible with the top down, and, to Samantha, he looked magnificently wild and tortured. The deaf guy still sat there, silently complicit with her dad's quick exit three years before.

Today Samantha stood on the sloshy beach, her long, straight blonde hair tickling the skin of her back left bare by her swimsuit. She watched the mud ooze over the tops of her new, white J.C. Penny Keds and thought about her counselor, Pamela, and how nice she was. Pamela had short black hair cut into choppy layers that framed her round face and kind brown eyes with blunt, thick lashes. The first night of camp Pamela had asked Samantha questions like, "What did you think of the colors of the sunset?" or "Do you like chocolate ice cream? If not, can I get you a piece of strawberry pie?"

Samantha had stared back at her counselor in a kind of mute wonder at being asked such things. It wasn't just the asking. It was the way she asked, with such patience and care, as if Pamela really wanted to know what lived inside of her.

Samantha had known that she liked Pamela as soon as she saw Pamela's big, warm smile shining at her on the first day of camp. When Pamela walked straight up and announced that she would be Samantha's counselor, Samantha was elated. Then Pamela put a tanned muscular arm around Samantha's shoulder and grabbed the young girl's suitcase.

"Come on, I'll take you to the cabin. You must be tired after your bus ride. Was it about four hours?"

"Yes, I think so." Samantha answered dutifully.

"Is this your first time at camp?"

Samantha's bright forest-green eyes widened. "Yes," she said nervously.

Pamela laughed, "Don't worry, you'll be fine. This is my second year as a counselor and before that I came here as a camper. I'll keep an eye on you. I used to be really shy too until a few years ago. I guess because I discovered sports and boys."

Samantha giggled at her counselor's flirty comment. It didn't even bother her that Pamela guessed that Samantha was introverted.

"I guess it won't be so bad. It sure smells good," Samantha said.

"Those are the eucalyptus trees. I love the way the scent gets into your nostrils and you can't help but take a big, yummy breath."

"Yeah, it does," said Samantha as she drew the fresh air in through her nose, feeling a gentle happiness rise in her chest.

Samantha couldn't stop smiling the whole day: through orientation; her lunch of fried chicken, mashed potatoes and green beans; the introductory hike to the lake; and the evening's BBQ, bonfire and songfest that followed. Pamela was mindful of Samantha the entire time, giving her a quick smile or wink whenever their eyes met.

Samantha could barely sleep that first night on the flat springy mattress flopped like a thin layer of skin on top of the hard bunk bed. It wasn't the mattress that kept her eyes open until the sun bored through the cabin window the next morning. It was the sheer joy and wonder at her counselor's behavior that made her feel as if she might run out of breath. She had to keep reminding herself to inhale down to her belly so she wouldn't hyperventilate and maybe even faint.

Faint like she did that day at the mall when a cute, older boy had passed her by and exclaimed how gorgeous she was. All the blood had rushed to her head and then drained back out in a heartbeat, so that she couldn't breathe. She got dizzy, and suddenly a security guard was standing above her body, which was now rolled out on the busy shopping walkway. It was the attention that was so disturbing, from a boy who had seemed absolutely taken with something about her she didn't recognize.

This time she was determined to accept the special notice from her counselor, even if it meant staying up that first night in a quiet labor of birth, breathing life into the good esteem she imagined for herself—convincing herself that she was worthy.

It helped that she was hundreds of miles away from the raven-ous eyes of her mother, watching, ever-watching for dangerous signs of people singling her out and giving her compliments. Like the time Samantha had come to the dinner table wearing a new red-gingham dress that fit snugly around her waist and flared out in a little skirt above her knees. Samantha's Aunt Zoe was visiting and she made a soft whistling sound.

"You sure are a beautiful girl, Samantha."

Samantha had blushed, trying to conceal the smile she felt be-ginning to curl the corners of her lips.

Sure enough her mother's face tightened into a hard frown as she poured herself another glass of wine. "Sit down, Samantha. We've already started dinner without you because you took so long primping yourself."

Samantha noticed that there was already an empty bottle of wine sitting on the table. At least her mother wasn't slurring her words—yet.

"Well, I think a pretty girl should be told that she is, at least once in a while," said her aunt, as she winked at Samantha.

"Thank you, Aunt Zoe, it's not necessary," Samantha mumbled.

She had already figured out how to deflect any note of special-ness headed her way. This kept her mother's fears and anxieties from burrowing too deeply inside Samantha's soft freckled skin. Still, it was confusing to Samantha, *what was so bad about it?*

Those first days at camp, Samantha felt free letting in the intox-icating draft of attention Pamela wanted to give her. Samantha detected that her counselor was experiencing as much joy as Samantha was in their new, special friendship. They often held hands—as they sang the camp songs that Pamela was teaching Samantha—all the way from the cabins past the arts and crafts hall, to the cafeteria and another half mile to the lake. Other coun-selors would smile at them with an amused nod of their heads.

Samantha hadn't felt this happy and alive for a long time. It all seemed incredibly simple. She didn't even have to do anything extraordinary for this magical feeling to continue pulsing through her from head to toe.

As the week continued, she and Pamela became even closer. The difference in their ages didn't matter. Samantha felt that someone finally recognized the self she had kept safe in her secret thoughts and dreams, the self she knew existed, but had only seen in her imagination, until now.

Pamela shared things with Samantha about her life at home, and how she could become angry and frustrated with how much her mother depended on her because there wasn't a man around the house. Pamela's father had died when Pamela was seven years old.

Samantha had been without a father for three years, and she knew the feeling of being smothered by a single parent. She would nod her head and sigh occasionally, as Pamela would talk with great force and animation. Samantha was a good listener from living with her mother, who constantly needed Samantha's attention to vent her many resentments, including the ones directed at Samantha's father. This had channeled a worldly wisdom into Samantha's small body.

Sometimes, when Samantha's mother had been talking for a long time Samantha began to feel invisible. It was like she was nothing—no feeling, and no presence, only a horrible awareness of her nothingness. It was as if she was an empty shell lying on a beach listening to the constant, droning wave of sound rushing back and forth, back and forth—her mother talking on and on.

But listening to Pamela was much nicer. Samantha didn't quite know why, except that she could feel herself as something real and separate. Maybe it was because Pamela laughed a lot and didn't rely on Samantha to make her feel good, like when her mom would talk and get annoyed with Samantha if she got restless or looked bored.

Or maybe it was because Pamela was interested in Samantha's thoughts and feelings too, unlike her mom. Samantha could listen to her mom for hours, and when it was her turn to talk, her mother would have to get up and do something, like get the laundry, make a phone call, or start dinner.

One night at camp, Pamela let Samantha walk with her to the restroom after lights-out. She said there was something she wanted to share with Samantha.

Samantha felt apprehensive waiting for Pamela to start talking, as small rocks on the trail poked against the bottoms of her Keds.

"I hope I didn't make you nervous or anything," Pamela said, "I just wanted to tell you something I wished somebody had told me when I was your age."

"Sure, go ahead," Samantha tried to sound nonchalant.

"I bet you feel things that you can't explain. Am I right?" asked Pamela.

"What do you mean?"

"Like sometimes you might know what other people are feeling, or thinking, without them telling you."

"Yeah, I guess so. You mean, like when I can tell my mom is sad, but she makes jokes instead?" Samantha wondered.

"Exactly! Do you ever feel that you can hear her thoughts?"

"All the time. Sometimes it's like the words she wants to say are hanging in the air and I can feel them. I pretend that I don't, though, because it makes her angry when I say something about it."

"Yeah, I know, I'm like that too. It just means that you're intuitive and sensitive to things."

Samantha dropped her head down. "Everyone says that I'm *too* sensitive. Even my doctor says that it might be why I faint sometimes, because I can get overwhelmed with too many feelings."

"Really?" Pamela seemed curious. "Are you asthmatic?"

"No, just really *sensitive*," Samantha's tone made it clear that she was making a joke at her own expense.

Pamela giggled in appreciation, "Well, maybe you wouldn't faint if you realized that it's okay to be sensitive, and to feel things. In fact, it is a special gift that you have. I have it too, and you can trust those feelings. You can trust what you know inside. I mean it! Listen to yourself and believe what you hear."

Suddenly Samantha didn't know where to put her hands. She felt self-conscious of her body, as if it was as big as an elephant's, monstrous and scary, but also powerful, like maybe she could actually beat Lori Martin at tetherball. She fixed her widening, wonder-struck eyes squarely on Pamela and put her hands in her pockets in an attempt to focus on the enormity of what was being revealed to her. *Come to find out that something she'd always been ridiculed for might actually be a kind of superpower.* Her eyes stung with emotion, and she almost ran into the restroom door, not noticing that they had reached their destination.

Pamela laughed. "You're funny, Samantha."

"You can call me Sam. That's what all my friends call me. Well, my friend Julie, my mom, and my dad, when he calls."

"Glad to be included on the list. Hey, Sam, do you want to try my mascara?"

"Sure, thanks, Pamela!"

"It's Pam. All my friends call me Pam."

They laughed with the mutual good feelings of their deepening bond.

"I've been spending a lot of time with Ryan," Pamela continued. "You know, the good-looking counselor with the tattoo that goes all the way down his arm."

"Oh yeah, I've noticed him. His arms are really sexy. I like the way the muscles in them are long and lean," Samantha said, feeling daring and grown up.

Pamela laughed. "He's sexy, all right. He's been sneaking over late at night, and I meet him at the canoe shed. Don't tell anyone, okay?"

"Absolutely not," Samantha assured her.

"I mean we haven't gone all the way. He just feels me up."

"Feels you up?"

"Yeah. You know, he puts his hand underneath my bra and touches my breasts. It feels good, actually, especially when we're kissing."

Samantha looked down at her flat chest, with its small pillowy nipples, and wondered if she'd ever have the right stuff to make a boy want to do that to her.

"We better go back, Sam. That mascara makes your eyes look amazing. You can keep it, if you want. I packed a new one in my luggage."

"Wow, thanks, Pam."

They walked back quickly to the cabin. Samantha felt so warm and happy inside that she didn't even notice the cold air.

But by the second week of camp, Samantha's counselor had become busy with extra work, as one of the other counselors had broken her foot after falling from a horse and had to go home. Pamela had no more time to pamper Samantha with attention, although she did still wink at Samantha whenever she passed her on a trail.

Samantha was disappointed, but in the meantime, she had found attention from a more fascinating source—an older boy who was in one of the cabins across the lake. This was where the Moonridge campsite for boys was located, and every day they would canoe over to the girls' campsite for co-ed recreation.

It was one day during swim time that Samantha spotted Brad, already a full-fledged teenager of 13. He had hair bleached by the sun, and deep brown eyes flecked with tan and rust, that made Samantha think of the smooth, thick leaves that fell all around their car when she and her family had driven through Connecticut one vacation. That was back in the days when her life matched those of her friends from school, who had both a mother and father living in the same house.

Brad noticed Samantha, too, and kept staring at her with those eyes that reminded her of a time when she felt secure and happy. Samantha finally smiled at him in spite of herself, and that's when Brad became unstoppable.

For the next few days he would come straight to Samantha, no matter what she was doing. She would raise her head above the cool protecting lake-water and there he'd be, dogpaddling, beaming at her. Once she was sitting with a group of nerdy boys, where there was no risk of the chest-stabbing fear that made her speech-less when Brad was around. Brad sauntered over and sat down so close to her that she could feel his wet swim trunks stick to her thigh.

"You're awful quiet all the time. Are you shy?" Brad spoke directly to Samantha.

She felt her cheeks getting hot, thinking that was a blunt thing for him to say, considering they had never had a conversation before.

Brad didn't wait for an answer from Samantha, but kept his eyes on her while he started telling the boys at the picnic table about a new video game his dad had sent him. She was amazed by his cheekiness and wondered if there was something wrong with him–something undetectable and sinister, like he was a psychotic or sociopath. Samantha knew these conditions from the endless Lifetime movies that she watched with her mother, once for an entire weekend, when they ran the "Tainted Love Movie Marathon." She knew that countless evil, weak men did horrible things to their wives and girlfriends and wondered if maybe Brad was one of those types. It was easier for her to think of it that way rather than acknowledge what she really feared: Brad would open up something wonderful in her 12-year-old heart and then walk away from her, just like her father.

Still, it was exhilarating that she could be sitting on the warm piney bench with her thin, muscled legs shooting out of her bright orange-and-red beach towel as these crazy thoughts raced through her mind. And Brad still looking at her and smiling, as though it didn't matter what she said or did. He just liked her.

At one point Brad leaned in and whispered in her ear, "I saw you blush. That's sweet. We should go for a walk sometime. I know where there's a little waterfall I could show you."

"Oh, I don't know about that," Samantha said, but she felt herself smiling.

Brad stood up and said to the group, "See you guys," then he winked at Samantha and walked away.

On the third day of this heady treatment, Samantha began to feel like the pretty girl that her teachers and the parents of her friends would tell her she was–basically, most of the adults in her life except for her mother. Now she started doing things she didn't even know she was capable of. She'd smile coyly at Brad and dip her head down so that the fall of her hair would angle over one eye. Then she'd fling her head back to whip the same hair over her shoulder, smiling again at Brad as if she possessed some great secret, but really there was not a thought in her head. Just this feeling of joy and warmth in her heart while her skin wouldn't stop tingling.

By the fourth day, the fear she had felt around Brad was completely gone. She agreed to take a walk with him to the cafeteria for a special co-ed lunch. She felt lighter when she walked and more coordinated, even graceful. She started skipping ahead to turn around, walking backwards while she faced Brad, aware of his amusement about this. There was this tension between them, as if they were holding opposite ends of an imaginary rope, and when one tugged an end the other felt it.

During their lunch of mesquite-grilled hamburgers and home fries, Brad kept trying to tickle Samantha's stomach and then under her arm. She liked the attention, but she had begun to feel annoyed. She was really hungry and it distracted her from eating.

"Brad, stop it!"

"No, I like getting you hot and bothered."

"Oh my gosh, Brad, please. People are looking." Samantha noticed that some of the kids near their table were watching them and laughing.

"Let 'em look."

"Brad, I'm serious," Samantha said under her breath, but then she started giggling.

"Made ya laugh," Brad said.

Samantha noticed that his eyes were a dark sparkling brown like they were lit with fire.

"Okay. Okay, I'll stop," said Brad," if you meet me tomorrow night after lights-out, at the canoe shed."

"Oh my gosh. I've heard about that place," Samantha said, while her thoughts were jumbling in her head. *I'm hungry. The canoe shed. Pam goes there to be felt up. I wish Brad would stop tickling me so I could think straight.*

"Come on, Samantha. It might be the last time I get to see you. We're heading home on Saturday," Brad lowered his eyes and looked up at her like a puppy dog waiting for a treat.

"Okay!" Samantha blurted, "I'll meet you, but just for a little bit. Just to say good-bye."

"Deal." Brad stopped tickling her and turned his body to finish his hamburger.

The next night, Samantha pretended to fall asleep immediately. After a torturous hour, she finally whispered through the cold cabin air, "Is anybody awake?"

Nothing. No sound except the usual snoring from Suzie Millhouse, who had a sinus condition.

Samantha grabbed the duffel of clothes she had stuffed at the foot of her sleeping bag and slipped out of the cabin, walking quietly to the nearby outhouse. Once she had changed, remembering to brush her eyelashes with some of the mascara that Pamela had given her, she started running. She heard a screeching owl calling through the thick night and her heart beat even faster. *I should have brought a flashlight!* She continued on by a thin glimmer of light from the crescent moon. The adrenaline pumped through her muscles and took away the usual nagging worries that plagued her daily–her flat chest and the idea that the popular girls at school were talking about her when she walked by. Then there was the persistent fear that her mother might die from the contents of all those vodka bottles that kept popping up like eggs on a hunt: in the laundry basket, behind the kitchen sink trash, and once, when the toilet wouldn't flush properly, Samantha had even found an empty bottle in the tank.

But tonight, as Samantha sprinted with Brad now in sight, she felt invincible from anything gloomy touching her world again.

She skidded to a stop, giggling as Brad pulled her by the waist and planted a fat kiss on her chin.

"Missed," Brad whispered, as he slid his tongue into her mouth. It felt thick and slimy and Samantha thought of a water slug she had once seen underneath the tomato patch in her mother's garden. She'd seen enough PG movies to know this was not the attitude she should be shooting for, so she tried to moan like those screen woman. Brad stopped. "Are you okay?"

"Um-hum, just cold," she answered.

"Come on," he said grabbing her hand and leading her into a damp shed that smelled like wet socks. The odor made Samantha's spirits drop and she started to feel the familiar knife of doom, which usually hung inside her chest. She suddenly noticed how all of that running and kissing in the raw mountain air was making it difficult to breathe. *Oh God, please don't let me faint.*

Brad started to pull her shirt up and it felt like the cabin was spinning around her. She suddenly wanted to get out of there, her heart beating, *go, go, go.* She felt like she was drifting outside of her body while Brad was busy undressing her actual body. It was like one of those dreams where she could fly over everything. She watched from above where the canoes hung like army bunks as Brad opened the metal button of her Levi Strauss low-rise flares. She saw herself standing as he took a scissor step, trapping her with his legs while his hand started to burrow down her white cotton panties. He was kneading and gnashing over her pubic bone until two of his fingers slipped up the hole inside of her.

I should do something, thought Samantha, as Brad eased her down on her back. She realized that she was lying on top of Brad's jacket. *When did he put that there? He's very skilled at this.* He'd now gotten her jeans and panties down around her knees, again without her awareness. *I'll have to pay more attention,* Samantha thought as something hard and foreign was trying to push into her body, into the soft, silent folds of her vagina, which hadn't even passed menstrual blood yet. Whatever it was, it seemed too big for her, dumb and unfeeling.

She couldn't move or talk. It was as if she was comatose while the whole rape took place. *Was it rape if you didn't fight or scream? What was it if you didn't say no, but you didn't say yes either?*

She was afraid to make him unhappy. She was afraid to lose the attention and feeling like she mattered to somebody. She was afraid to be alone on the walk back to her cabin. Suddenly the rock-like force jamming against her bones stopped.

"You're too small," Brad hissed, "Let me put it in your mouth."

That's when a pure bolt of female survival instinct hit her, probably from the same part of the brain that had allowed Delilah to enfeeble Samson, and Cleopatra to defeat an empire. She lied. Without any tremor or weakness in her voice she said she was going to throw up. She knew this gross admission would turn Brad off and he'd lose interest in conquering her body. Now all she had to do was get up and get out of sight so she could pretend she was vomiting.

She was now fully in her body, no longer split from heart and mind. She sprung up with the same might that had given her first place in the girls broad-jumping competition at school. She was pulling up her pants as she passed Brad, whose fuddled look almost made her laugh. She pushed the shed door open and gasped at the fresh air as if cresting the ocean's surface after a near drowning. It took her only three seconds to decide that she had to make a run for it. She bolted, and her feet barely touched the ground. It was remarkable, this surge of life and freedom in her body, her glorious, familiar and, once again, solely her own body. She heard herself laugh, and the release of it actually seemed to be a real thing that mingled with the icy air and raced beside her. When she saw the logged rectangular rise of her cabin, relief washed through her body as she realized she had been running for her life.

The Jaunt

by Bruce Moody

He had to get out of town.
For weeks he felt the need.
Get out under the trees.

Amble, wander, get lost.

When he went down to see if the mail had come, he found Beven wandering around the lobby.

"What the hell are you still doing here?"

"My ride had to have a fender replaced."

This ride to his retreat was to have picked Beven up two days ago, but the shop retained the man's car. For two days he had noticed Beven still here, looking flummoxed, adrift.

"I'll take you!"

"What? You can't take me."

"Of course I can, I'll bring my car around to the back entrance. You bring your stuff there, and we'll be off." Perfect. A two-hour drive. An escapade!

He got his car, backed in, opened the trunk.

He went down the hall and found Beven still in a fluster. He grabbed a sleeping bag, two duffle bags, a satchel, a folding chair he had lent Beven, and Beven said, "You can't do this."

"I want you to have a good time!"

"I couldn't ask you to."

"You didn't ask me to." He made off down the hall, Beven right after him, to the trunk of the station wagon where he tossed everything.

"Don't squeeze that like that!" Beven pulled out his favorite bag and took it to the passenger seat.

"Don't be cross," and he opened the rear door. "Before we go, you might call your car ride and cancel." He lowered the favored bag dutifully into the back seat.

Beven called.

Off they went!

He wanted to skirt Independence Day traffic, but they were captured. He thought, Would we keep our tempers? Ah, yes, we would. Traffic would be part of it.

They agreed to ditch the freeway and take the route around town. Whee!

No traffic!

Once over the bridge and in San Rafael, they needed to pee. At the service station he asked the mechanic where he could get lunch. Half a block away, what good luck!

Once there, Beven sat in the car while he went in and ordered to-go tunas on rye and while he waited ate a slice of homemade pie, which as An Internationally Known And Currently Sitting Secretary General Of The Pie-Taster Registry Of The World, (PTROTW) he knew was his bounden duty to not disregard.

"While I eat this, would you drive?"

So Beven took the wheel and complained about the wide rear-view mirror.

"Nothing I can do about it."

"Can it not be so blue?"

Maybe things were not quite as Beven desired. But Beven said no more.

The mechanic said to make a U-turn to get back on the freeway, but the sign slashed the U. Had he himself been driving, he might have made the turn, but Beven said, "I'll go left and come round." He remained, though pie-faced, alert to what sort of a driver Beven was.

He was reassured. Beven was a correct driver.

The traffic ten miles an hour—but the heck with it—they were on their way. A jaunt isn't a jaunt if you make yourself miserable. So he was happy.

Beven was a slightly bent man with a paltry mustache and a pinched face. Humor lurked under it like a hungry fish under a lily. The corners of his eyes flowered when he smiled. Pinched, he figured, was a product of Beven's age. Age gives faces masks that don't necessarily reveal interiors. Age is mainly Gravity pulling you down to earth. Age is grave, however you spell it. For Beven was kind, shrewd, and politically open regarding The Residents Council Meeting in the low-income senior housing where they lived. For an hour they talked its politics, to escape which was one reason why he'd wanted to get out of town to start with.

"One thing about you, Beven, is that you and I are in accord about The Residents Council. You're a bit ahead of me on the road, but I'm not far behind."

"The first two words you ever said to me, I knew we were on the same side," said Beven. He could hear that Beven was glad to have said this, and for it to be true. Back home, they were going to win everything without appearing even to fight for it.

Nothing more was said on the matter. They were not ones to gossip. Gossip would have made them unhappy. And it would have brought into play nothing that could be solved in the car or maybe at any other time, even by their own agency.

So they drove in a concord of silence.

Presently, he looked at Beven's profile. He wondered if Beven felt as at-ease as he was.

"How do you feel?"

"Disgruntled." Beven meant about the missed two days.

"Will you have to pay for them?"

"I called ahead, and they let me off. I had a scholarship anyhow. Actually I'll get some money back."

"Is disgruntledom going to give you a good time?"

"No, it's not," admitted Beven and got off it.

He loaded the CD player with Johnny Hartman but didn't turn it on. If Beven wanted to hear it, good. If not, good. Hartman was a recent find, like the fruit pie.

He pulled the seat lever and like a Morris Chair the seat fell back. In it he reclined for his post-pie nap.

~~~~~

He woke.

They were way out in the country.

"How long was I asleep?"

Beven hadn't been timing it.

"I always nap twenty minutes. Still traffic I see."

"I almost turned back."

He wondered how Beven could allow mere traffic to dampen such a lark. He didn't ask. He wondered about Beven's stick-to-it-iveness. He didn't ask. He'd find out. He'd only known Beven for five months. This was their first adventure.

Beven was Gay and declared as such. Beven's retreat was a Gay retreat. Beven had looked forward to it, had been there before. Don't nag Beven about saying he might give up on the retreat. Nagging isn't going to give either of us a good time.

He looked out at the scenery.

It was nice to be chauffeured in one's own car.

The freeway was now two lanes.

"There's a bottleneck." Beven could see ahead. "They're controlling traffic. I can see police lights."

The accident looked bad. Traffic had slowed for over an hour, but still, a man lay on the pavement. Medics knelt. Red ambulance. Another man down on the road. Others stood by. A car askew. Two motorcycles parked.

"Motorcycles," he said. "They frighten me to death. You can't hear them before they're on top of you."

Beven had worse to say. Sounded like Beven wanted to genocide them.

The traffic speeded back to 70.

"You want to listen to this?" he asked about the Johnny Hartman CDs. "We don't have to." He laughed at himself. He'd gotten to be such a good guy with old age.

"No, that's fine," said Beven, and they listened to Johnny Hartmann sing.

Beven listened closely. Beven had never heard of him. "Miss Otis Regrets"—Beven at first didn't like the lyric. At the end he liked it. Beven had never even heard The American Songbook. "They all sound the same to me." So Beven, who listened not to the songs, but to the singing, remarked on Hartman's vocal range.

Interesting. Beven's appreciation was technical.

"And perfect intonation," he offered Beven.

But he wanted to leave Beven alone with it, so he didn't say what he really got in Hartman. Masculinity. Co-ordination of the singer with his instrument. Everything natural. Nothing forced or showy. Ease. Command. Variety. In the moment. Richness. Absence of virtuosoism. Flexibility. Bass-baritone. Beauty, simple beauty. A singer apart.

"And he sounds as though he's actually singing to somebody," he blurted out as though this were the most important thing.

Beven said Hartman sounded like Joe Williams.

"Who's that?"

Beven said he'd lend him some.

The drive was easy.

And fast.

Beven got close to the car in front. Going seventy means seven car spaces, so he said something, and Beven held back.

"That's all right. You're a good driver." He knew he would not have gone to sleep had Beven been not.

"I love this valley," said Beven.

He looked about not seeing anything to love.

"It reminds me of Hawaii."

He had never been to Hawaii, but he never imagined Hawaii looked like this, this color green, these very skies, hills. He said nothing.

Beven was an individual of passions hidden beneath the surface of a mild and taciturn exterior. Beven was moved by the life he had lived. It was precious to him. He was meticulous about it. Beven spoke of these places with a feeling he had never seen Beven bare.

So he set aside his talent to killjoy the Hawaii comparison and let Beven be.

When they started, he had said to Beven what he said to all his passengers: "Beven, I want you to understand that we drive this car by consensus. If I am doing something you don't like. If I am about to kill the old lady, remind me. Going too fast for ya? Say so. I will not take offense."

It was true to how he lived now, and how he lived at the place he lived, and how it is true in friendship as it is formed. If theirs was forming, it depended as much upon what was said as upon what was not said. Friendships begin and run on an unspoken consensus.

And, because he liked to look at maps, he opened one.

"We could go on Route 8."

"Winding road. Twice as long."

"When I leave you off, I'm going to take these backroads. And maybe get out and swim. I got my trunks in the trunk."

They left the freeway and drove on a blue road past lakes, one after another, that he never knew were there.

After that, Beven knew exactly how to go, where to turn. Left, up a lane.

On the left, a paddock. Magnificent horses.

"Do you ride those horses?" he asked Beven.

"No."

"Say, 'No,' again just like that."

Beven laughed.

"No."

"No. Not like that. Like before."

"No," he said.

"Perfect," he said.

They drew past a dirt parking lot. A stark-naked middle-aged man with a fat dangling cock stared at them as they passed.

"That man's stark naked."

"You'll see a lot of that here."

He wanted to get back and get close. Which, after all, was why the man was naked, wasn't it? For folks to look at his cock closely?

They drove slowly into the compound, parked by a chainmail fence, beyond whose gate Beven needed to hunt for a place to set up his tent.

When Beven found a fine place in the shade, he helped Beven pile up his camping things next to a tree. He wanted to get back to the cock in the parking lot.

"Before you set up your tent could you show me around?"

Would the cock still be there? He wanted to hurry things along.

So they left the tent not set-up and parked the car in the center of the compound. Then Beven showed him around the retreat center.

He pressed his brow to the pane of The Hall Of Healing. Inside, a workshop wrapped up. Twenty naked senior males lay about in tangles of post-workshop languor. In the middle, two nude men stood and kissed strongly. He stared at them. Would the cock still be there? Unlikely. To distract himself, he looked at the kissing men.

They walked across the lawn.

"A lot of swinging dicks around here."

"I thought you'd be used to that," said Beven.

"No. I'm not." No, he wasn't comfortable. He didn't like that he liked what he liked. Even here, he didn't want anybody to know.

For sure.

On the way to the lodge, Beven told him this retreat center had been open since the '80s. He had been going here since the '90s. It seemed odd to him that Beven, such a quiet type, would go to such a bold place.

Men came up to greet Beven. Beven introduced him as the man who had driven him up here but was not a member. "Well maybe you'll become a member," one said. "You'll stay for dinner," another said. "We'll put you up for the night," said another. "That's the least we can do for bringing him here."

They were playful in their pressure. They were hospitable. They were at ease in being here.

Here.

What was here?

Here was a place where Gay men could gather in the conceit of having convincingly admitted themselves to the status of everyone present. They were middle-aged. They were old. They were Gay. They were out; they needed a place. A village not near any other village. A village where they would not be stoned.

He had been stoned. But he had never been comfortable in Gay communities. He had sampled them. They were not his home—even though he still wanted to get to that dick.

For Beven this place was not artificial, but for him, this place was artificial. Poised. He was content not to proclaim it. It is a sin to violate hospitality. He let Beven lead him along.

Back in the old folks home where they lived, Beven did not disguise he was gay. The only dissonance between them was Beven's persistence that he too belonged to this club. But Beven's insistence wouldn't make it so. Persuasion wouldn't make it so. Joining up wouldn't make it so.

He had had plenty of sex with men. That didn't make it so either.

And yet he wanted to see the dicks and he knew it. He was not Gay with a capital G. But rather on a sexual spectrum, in which wanting to see dicks certainly was included. And here they were on display. For sex?

Or was it for something else?

Access to a masculinity otherwise denied?

Or just to see dick! To see it!

"I'd like to see the pool." He'd see dicks there. He would never tell Beven.

In the pool, lounging on chaises and floating on backs and standing in water, talking and joking, stood fifteen portly naked males. He and Beven remained clothed, and from the secrecy of the shade of his broad-brimmed hat his scurried looks saw dicks. Saw them and sought to see them.

He checked them out. He hoped he hid that he checked them out. He wanted to see what everyone had. But he wanted to elude the weakness that being seen to be seeking to see dicks betrayed. He kept in his closet at the same time as he peered through its keyhole.

As though he could not get his fill of it. Which he could not, since there is no such thing as a fill of it. Every single one of these fuckers was circumcised. Some sizeable members. Some pretty penises. No one was in shape.

No one was looking at anyone's. Was that intentional? Maybe being naked got them used to them. Or maybe that was an undress code. It was hard to know. For gay men often cackle at things as funny, although they know they aren't funny one bit. Sad laughter. You couldn't tell.

Staking a premium on his own hypocrisy, he took care to deliberately pass one white-haired man on a chaise but merely briskly glance between his legs. Nice dick. Fat. The man's eyes were angry and alone. He wanted to come back to that man and see more.

Beven took him to the big, empty Jacuzzi.

They sat on a long flat rock, and Beven told him how, after dark, this was a lively place. He knew just what would happen here. He knew if he stayed the night he would go here. He knew exactly what he would do. He would do everyone. "It's a great place to see the stars," said Beven.

The stars is not what he would see.

"This rock is hot," said Beven and they got up.

The dinner bell had rung.

Everyone drifted toward the lodge.

But two arced scrims on the lawn stood in their way.

Before any of them could pass, a little man with a megaphone and a Jemima bandana over his pate hailed everyone and handed each a colored heart on a necklace string. When they'd put it around their necks, he handed them a pencil and a slip of colored paper to fill out what they wanted for the weekend and to pin it on the scrim.

"Follow The Leader," he heard. He wrote as he was bidden and pinned it on the scrim.

Then the Jemima man megaphoned for everyone to come from behind the scrim one by one and express themselves before everyone as to what they wanted for the weekend.

Express themselves? What did that mean? He'd watch.

Each man came out and threw his arms wide in a gesture of whatever feeling it was a gesture of. He watched them. Each did the same thing. Because each man had no imagination for it yet because each was willing to look foolish, each man got applause.

He felt happy. Everyone was nice to him here. And he always felt happy. Or almost always. And he had been happy to meet everyone he had met so far and happy to see what this place was and to be here in the land of the unexpected.

Do it, he said to himself. Follow the leader.

Don't charm them when your turn comes. Just be happy—which you are.

He came last out and stood. He took a long look at each and every one in turn. A big semi-circle of men. He rotated like a lighthouse. To let them see it. His happiness. A hundred men there. As he was. He let them in, as they were.

When he was done, he took off his big soft white-duck plantation hat and in a low bow to them swept it to the ground.

Then the Jemima man megaphoned them to group themselves by the colored heart around their necks. He joined Beven in the violet group. The Jemima man gave awards to each group, commended each for some silly something or other. His helper handed out little heart-centers for the missing cutout centers of the hearts each member wore. He applauded with the others as though he were already a member.

Announcements were made, for KP, rides, service, all informative, many funny. Any excuse to laugh. The easy air of July.

He liked it.

He and Beven walked up together for dinner.

"The guy with the megaphone thought he was so cute and funny," said Beven.

"He was cute and funny."

True, although, of course, the megaphone man did think he was cute and funny.

They were last on the dinner line, and, because he was tired of standing, he sat at a picnic table. Beven went for water, came back with the water, and got on the line for food, but he stayed sitting. Watching.

Most men wore a dhoti—something that could be whipped off for full Monte without stepping out of pants. The dhotis felt like a tradition of the place. At last, a dress! He wanted them to flip open then and there so he could see what they had.

These men looked prosperous, even when nude. Some formerly married. Out in a place they could be Out in, grandchildren notwithstanding. They could be here in a way they could not be at home. Beven too. Where they lived, Beven made no bones about being Gay, here it was not necessary to declare it, here it was understood.

He went inside and found Beven filling his plate. Only two pieces of chicken the sign said, and he obeyed.

Outside on the porch, Beven waved to him from a picnic table, keeping him under his wing. Good. He felt safe to be fostered by Beven. And, after all, he was but a guest.

Beven straddled the picnic table seat, which was too close to the table to get your leg over easily.

"Riding sidesaddle?" he said. But he got his leg over and sat.

The man opposite introduced himself. He had white hair, probably in his late sixties. He had a walker. He was glad to meet this man. But the man immediately looked at him. He knew what that particular look meant. He didn't want it.

This man was short, ordinary, daring. His husband was to sit next to him. He was marking time and making time until the husband came.

This husband turned out to be six-five, with night-black hair cascading down his back and chest, and the carved features of a woodsman. A big Paul Bunyan energy, one easy to get along with. He stationed a shopping bag on the table and from it he drew pill bottles, pretty as candy.

"I hope you brought enough for everyone," he said.

"I did," said Paul Bunyan. "Some of us forget to bring our meds." He took pills from the bottles and swallowed them. Paul Bunyan was with AIDS.

His attitude was hearty and ample. The pills really were for everyone. However, at one point, his white-haired husband told him to keep his elbows to himself. Bunyan dutifully tucked in his giant wings, made a funny face, but made no incident.

He figured the man with the walker kept the giant with AIDS, perhaps because of AIDS or perhaps because the giant was an impressive male. The giant was happy. The man with the walker was not happy.

He liked the giant, but he didn't want to stay seated across from his husband. He didn't want to make the effort to skirt the look in the man's eyes, which was still in his eyes, despite the giant. So he kept his eyes lowered and ate.

He looked up and saw, over on the porch, scrawled on a huge brown paper a schedule of the weekend's events.

After diner, a dance. He knew what would happen. As the new boy he would be asked to dance and he would. And he would enter into the romantic energy of dance, as he always did, and that would lead to the Jacuzzi. And to what he would feel afterwards.

That much was certain.

The place was fine. It was dear. It was a haven. But not his. He had a style for sex, but this was not his style. It did not speak to him or for him. In fact, it spoke against him. Against his style.

That tall, thin man standing there wore a chrome bikini codpiece. Another in metal trousers, same pouch, but gold. Codpieces bright as mirrors. This was a place where everyone's package could be on neon display. He did not want to be on display. He was ashamed of his paunch, how he looked nude. How his cock had retreated into pre-adolescence. He didn't look old. But he was. Older probably than anyone here. He was 83.

He got up and took his dishes to the kitchen.

There a man came up to him and said, "Thanks for coming out and just standing there. That took some doing. Taking us all in. Are you in the theatre?"

"Yes, I am," he said.

"I appreciate you," the man said. "Thank you."

What should he have said?

He said, "You're very welcome."

What should he have said?

"I'm actually fourteen? But I have striven towards old age all my life. This ancient body you see before you is entirely manufactured. I'm not fat but slim. I appear six-two but I am five-five. You see these double chins. It took two-dozen procedures to get them. Under them, my jawline is impeccable. Since age six, I've done everything I could to looked geriatric. To embody the secret of perpetual old age. Did I say I am fourteen? A fib. Thirteen."

Of course, he wouldn't say that. That man wanted nothing from him save permission to praise.

He walked down the steps of the lodge and out on the neutral lawn. Daylight still held its conversation. The green trees. The blue sky.

Perfect.

Stay?

Go?

Stay?

He had followed the leader. Whether the leader was Beven or the place itself or what it offered, he had followed, and with a merry will followed. Now he would go home. Now he would follow something else.

Beven pressed, "Well, are you going to sign up?"

"I think I'll sleep at home, Beven."

"Oh, are you sure?"

"Beven, I thank you for everything. I had a grand time."

"Maybe one day."

As they stood there, the man who had promised Beven a ride drove up. Beven had a way home. He could leave him safely taken care of.

He got in his car.

Beven opened the passenger door and took his shirt meticulously from the front seat. Beven forgot nothing.

Then he came to the driver's door.

He held out a bill.

"What?"

"Can I give you twenty dollars?"

"For what?"

"I was going to give you money for gas."

"My treat. Free."

Beven didn't understand.

"I want you to have a good time, Beven."

Beven still didn't understand. Beven was under water in a pond he had long ago created.

He pulled out of the compound and drove past the magnificent horses—one of them big, shiny, black. The naked man was gone.

He would drive back by the lakes. A hundred miles? It was 7:45, high summer, plenty of daylight left. A two-hour ride here should take three hours back. He should get back before dark. It didn't matter anyhow. The jaunt was still on.

He turned left on 6 and then right on 11B, which, he saw by the map, went all the way to Calmath Station, a town he knew.

Then home.

He loved the long days of summer, July first, and exploring un-known country. What could be better?

Farms and ranches evolved on either side. A four-lane divided highway allowed him to drive his favorite 55 MPH. At his age, the way to be lawless was to obey the law.

The road wound and was trafficked lightly the other way. This was the way they should have come. 11B went almost to the door of the retreat center. He'll tell Beven for next time.

He had drunk a little glass of lemonade before he left, but he had no need to pee. He turned on Johnny Hartman. The Black Label of singers.

When the crossroads came, he slowed to make out 11B. So many roadside signs. To this town by this route, to that town by that. His gas tank was half-full. He was loaded. He was free.

The blue flank of Gemson Lake opened out on the left, and its town showed itself as a summer place. The wineries, which the big vineyards fostered, offered estate tours. The word "estate"—did it mean mansions or was it a got-up word to attract buyers to a tra-dition as though the vintners had been in operation since 1890 instead of 1990. He didn't care. Driving was the wine.

The road narrowed, so there was no looking to right nor to left. He drove south. The sun was going down from the west, so he had no trouble seeing.

He liked to drive. He wasn't going to stop at the State Park to swim. The water was too young not to be cold. He didn't even see a sign for it. Going to drive blue roads home.

Pear orchards. Pear orchards. Pear orchards.

At the Portmanteau turnoff, he slowed and drove straight across.

Two-lane that curved as it followed a creek. Farmhouses showed. A few behind trees. Cows. A yard-full of horses.

Then none.

Presently the yellow centerline stopped. He wondered at that, since 11B was a principal road in these parts.

I mean, he had friends who drove daily up from Calmath Station to Warren to work, a straight road, crowded at rush hour. Up here it was country, though. The last road sign had said 84 miles to Calmath.

When the farms vanished, he hadn't noticed it.

Then he did.

And kept on noticing it.

He found himself traveling through a haunted valley.

Empty, narrow, vagrant.

Up and down hills. Around 20 MPH corners.

On either side now scorched stems of young trees stood where the last summer wildfires had burned everything away and his friend Joe's house to the ground. Joe lived around here somewhere. At Vanish Lake? Or was it Centerville?

The little tree trunks still stood, and he wondered how those little trees, four feet tall, could have fueled such a famous fire.

The intermittent tall trees were black, naked, dead.

And yet not dead.

Green leaves were alive on the ends of sooty branches. Tall or short, those trees had outlived the conflagration. In Vanish County. Wilmott County. A national disaster. And he was driving through it. The trees had a life of their own. Dark green. Green as coal.

And yet ghosts.

For miles through this valley of ash, the road narrowed more and more.

He didn't understand it.

11B?

Maybe not travelled much hereabouts.

Or maybe he had not driven on 11B! Maybe the Portmanteau turnoff was not what it appeared. He had driven straight across the crossroads, thinking it must still be 11B. But maybe 11B had ended or turned.

The light was grey and uniform.

Over the steep, low hills, dusk lay supine in its gauzes.

The two-way road shrank to a single lane, and he realized no 11B sign had appeared on it, ever. He was going the wrong way.

No, he was not going the wrong way. He was going the right way. He was going south.

There was also no "No Outlet Sign." Yes, the road was odd. But it would debouch somewhere.

Anyhow it was too late to turn back. He had come this far. He had better keep going.

He was no longer happy.

Did he feel fear?

Perhaps—because happiness had been replaced by hope and hope by its poor relation, anxiety. Anxiety pedaled to the floor by impatience, which did not want him to be where he was, but elsewhere, elsewhere meaning the end, the outcome, the safety of a recognized way home.

The road was a moon of potholes. He drove carefully. He drove slowly. The road so narrow, so many turns. Scars, rises, declines.

Winding road next eleven miles.

He bumped along.

He knew the tires would hold because they were new. But he knew no aid would come to him if he broke down. He had not passed a house for a long time. He had not passed a corral a cow, a barn, a fence.

And never a car.

Nor now did he expect to.

"Oh, God!" A rabbit scattered across the road just under the car wheels. But when he looked, no rabbit lay on the road.

His top speed now was 20 MPH. The road was odd. Bumpy.

Yet, although he'd tried to evade the potholes, now he saw there were no potholes. All the potholes had been paved. Their patches made the bumps.

He toiled on. Where was he? Why no human habitation? No crossroads? Why did no one live on it? Who did this road belong to? The Forest Service?

Road flooded next six miles.

Rain had not fallen for three months. He would be fine.

The car drove down into a vale. At its basin lay a flat white concrete bridge over a dead creek. Over it the creek would rush when rain fell. Cars would portage across.

The night went on and the road went on and Johnny Hartman went on—beautiful, accomplished, warm. As though in Manhattan's Café-Society. In the dark. Not this dark. Another dark. He paid no attention to Johnny Hartman.

A panther leaped across the road and disappeared into its own black shadow in the trees.

No deer.

No birds.

No stopping.

When will this end?

Barely drivable. No parlor light. No hint of an end.

Nothing to do but drive this creek-shaped road.

This scullery maid of roads.

Around corners, up hills, down dales.

Tedious.

But not tedious. Because he had to drive watchfully.

But being watchful was tedious too.

Careful, pal. Be watchful about the tedious.

He slowed.

He stopped.

Ahead the asphalt tilted, cracked, slid down the hillside into the creek.

The road had avalanched. In one continuous sheet, it tipped. But the top was still round. Just enough road left. Perhaps drivable.

So up it he drove, onto the peak of the asphalt, and it held. Across it. And down the other side and off.

Another winter rain, the road would wash into the ravine.

One after another low white concrete portage bridges, identical. After ten none.

Night was fully on.

The valley dark folded the road in.

The headlights steered the car, not he.

Don't stop.

If you stop, you die.

Cast away.

No one to rescue you.

That was what those retreat-men refused to be.

Castaway.

Each one was the other one's Friday.

But he?

He had his style.

And here he was. A night's lodging declined on a point of style.

But yes, yes, now there was nothing left for him but this wilderness.

In which he knew he dared not stop.

The road.

In the midnight dark.

Flattened out.

To a bluff.

Which achieved a cliff over a lake.

A huge lake. Where he stopped.

Lake Marigold.

In the light of stars he could see Marigold's sea. The largest lake in the state. Man-made. Marigold State Park.

He had swum in it in the days he did masters swimming.

He knew where he was.

The road widened.

With a yellow centerline.

On the right in turn-offs by lamplight, July 4th campers stood by their RVs.

And on the left, Day-Use-Only launch ramps and beaches barriered for night.

The lake was long, and he would have to drive the length of it.

There, below the black night, it gleamed with captured stars.

At each park sign he slowed to see if it meant there was a highway.

No. Each led to campgrounds.

Then the road turned right, no more lake.

Through black writhing woods.

Which would end where?

He must have driven this road years before. But he did not remember its particulars.

He arrived at a T.

He stopped.

Left to Warren.

He was still in the woods, but there was a streetlight. Now he was on the homestretch. Now he knew where to go.

He switched off Johnny Hartman. Parked. Turned on the overhead. Picked up the map. Yes, back there at Portmanteau 11B went right. This error road was the fortunate fall. The felix culpa. The unplanned. The unplanned terror by night.

He started the car up and went left.

A bar!

A bar?

In the middle of nowhere?

In the dead black and night of a forest!

Or what looked like a bar.

Or might be a grocery store.

Or a restaurant.

He pulled into the gravel and parked.

Neon suggested a bar.

Have a beer.

He wasn't a beer drinker. Why would he do this? It would add delay to his homecoming.

But he would do it. Stretch his legs. Stop. Talk to the first human beings in fifty miles. Stop because it was a place to stop. A jaunt means always to land in a strange place. To stop continuing. To stop the fear that paves the familiar. To stop. At the stumbled-upon. The don't-say-no-to.

He crossed the gravel.

Ahead, on a picnic bench under the overhang, he saw the black shadows of a man and woman gabbing in the pitch.

"Is this a bar?"

"Oh, honey, it sure is. Go on in and be welcome."

He pushed an old wood door.

Groceries on shelves.

To the right, chairs, Formica tables, a serving counter closing down.

To the left a bar.

Dollar bills hung above the bar. Glued up by one end, the other end drooping. Hundreds of bills. And all the way up the wall. Dollars. And behind the bar. Who could count? Dollar bills. All autographed. To the left and to the right. From the ceiling. Dollars.

Although certain bald spaces on the ceiling showed where time's gravity had had its way.

No one was at the bar.

Dismay.

But a barman at the far end put things away for the night.

He walked up, took a stool, and sat.

An old man with curly blond hair came in and a woman followed him and stood at the bar at the far left of him. They gabbed and laughed. The barman came down to them. He could hear little the three said. "You're not allowed in this place?" he heard the barman say, and the three laughed as though nothing could be further from the truth. The barman handed a case of beer over to them.

When do you close?" he said.

"When the tide goes out," said the barman. He was tall, maybe mulatto, heavyset, nice looking, a small mustache. Part Japanese maybe. Cute. The discretionary bachelor. Should I make a move?

"What do you have on draft?'

"Bottled only."

"Any dark beer?"

The barman named the most famous. But he had already had the most famous. The barman named the second most famous.

"I'll have that. I've never had that before."

The barman put the new beer before him. Its glass perspired. The label said, "Bottled in England."

He poured it into a frosted pilsner glass and said:

"The most amazing thing just happened to me. I was driving down from Gemson Lake on 11B and I found myself on this strange road. There was nothing on it. For miles. Not a house. Not a ranch. Not even another car. This thin tiny road. Through burned trees. I thought it would never end."

The barman's voice was weary. "Desolate," he said.

By the way the barman said this word, he knew the barman knew the road.

"Desolate," he affirmed. "Spooky."

The barman went about his business. Too much trouble to put the make on him.

No. Not enough juice in him to turn the trick.

On a plate on the counter behind the bar sat what looked like an old eggroll.

"Is there any food at the bar?"

Why did he ask this? He had already eaten.

"Eggrolls and Polish sausage."

"Polish sausage."

The barman went about preparing it.

The barman put before him a mustard jar, a relish jar, a jar of chopped onions, big plastic ketchup upside down.

"Eggrolls any good?" he asked as though to order those too.

"Best in the world," the barman said as though for the thousandth time.

But they wouldn't go with beer.

The barman split a roll and brought the Polish sausage.

Two women came in and sat along to his left. The older black-haired woman on this side. The younger? Because of her curly hair, not possibly her daughter. It was hard to tell, because the bar was dark, as bars are.

They ordered, and the barman brought a can of something to the younger, and before the older he placed a black shot glass and poured into it.

The woman raised it to her lips, took a sip, and shuddered destructively.

"I want you to come over and fix my lawnmower."

"I fixed the last one. What's with you and lawnmowers?" said the barman good-naturedly.

"That belonged to the Willards. This one's mine."

"You're hard on lawnmowers."

"I was just using it. There's all these springs. I have no idea where they go. You've got to come over. You've got a way with lawnmowers."

He heard this as he ate. But he was not part of it. He also heard the barman say, "When I pick my kids up from school." And then he really knew he was not part of it.

The older woman was in her early fifties and good looking. Slender. Rich dark black hair pulled behind her ears. Flowing down her back past her shoulders. Sharp featured.

"They took away our land, and this is what they left us," she said to the young woman and the barman. She was in a good humor. What was she talking about? She was attractive. Should he pick her up?

"They called us Indians. Then those other Indians took our name away. Now we're called Native Americans. But we still call ourselves Indians. Indjins."

"Injuns" said the young woman.

"No. Indjins." She turned to him. "That's what they do," she said to him. "Take away. I don't care, but they took everything away from us, and now that."

"When I was young," he said, "they called American Indians Indians, and the others East Indians."

She turned to him. "Yes, East Indians." She wasn't drunk. Or even beginning drunk. She was Indian but she was clear of it. So far.

Finished his sausage and swallowed his beer down and gave the barman a credit card. $8.24. Didn't seem like much. He put two dollars on the counter.

He stood to go.

"I've seen you somewhere," the older woman said.

And the young woman stood up and looked at him. So did the

barman.

"Yes, I've seen your picture," she said.

They hadn't seen my picture. There was no picture.

"It's true," he said as he stood there for them. He said what he said because he liked them and because he was happy again.

"There's lots of pictures of me. You see them. Magazines. Newspapers. It's been like that. The thing is, though, I change my name all the time. Everyone knows me, but no one can identify me. Lots of pictures, but the name's always different. So useful. I recommend it."

They were speechless with incredulity. Amused with incredulity.

"Have a happy Fourth."

He meant it. It was an exit line. He went out the door and felt great.

He got in the car and sat.

He had done well in there. Given good value. Was there something he might have added? But it was too late. Never mind. He'd been jaunty. That was his style—imagination. That's what people wanted. They'd never forget him. That was enough. He would never forget them.

Johnny Hartman sang, and off he went. Stopped dead at every crossroad to be sure the sign was right. It always was.

He drove to Warren. Then down to Calmath Station.

He picked up gas at his favorite place and in half an hour pulled up at his old peoples' home under the redwoods where he lived.

He had run out of Johnny Hartman by then. He looked at his watch. 11:45. Return trip four hours.

Good.

Very good.

Excellent mischances.

To amble. To get lost. Find one's way home.

Yes, true, the road signs were hard to read.

But there they were.

Authors

Merrilee Cavenecia

Merrilee Cavenecia, while retired from a career in education and anthropology, has had a lifelong love of writing. She is currently active in the Benicia Literary Arts community, where she belongs to writing groups focused both on poetry and prose. She is currently writing a novel on immigration as well as writing memoirs of meaningful events in her life, including this piece on the baptism of a Lacandon Maya baby.

Judea Cavoto

I have been writing stories since I was a child growing up in East Bay, California. I feel writing to be a natural act of listening within, and honoring a truth that is seeking to be seen, or heard. "A Dark Night at Moonridge Camp" was inspired by a writing prompt, and continues to expand into a novel. I dedicate this story to the memory of Sandra Bisceglia-Jones, and the enduring power of friendship.

Grant Cooke

Grant Cooke is a businessman, journalist, and book author, with a focus on emerging technologies, renewable energy, and sustainability. He helped develop startups and early-stage businesses and designed energy efficiency programs for utilities in multiple states. Along the way, he published numerous articles and co-authored five books, including *The Green Industrial Revolution: Energy, Engineering and Economics*, the reference book for sustainability and carbonless economies. He has lived in Benicia for thirty years.

Tamar Enoch

I write with seven wonderful women in a group sponsored by Benicia Literary Arts. We gather two Fridays a month to share our work over coffee and cookies. Thanks to this group, I have written my way through three moves, three jobs, and a spiritual crisis. I have also learned to eschew adverbs and not to pass off prose as poetry. Thank you, Beth, Carolyn, Cyndi, Linda, Lisa, Lois, and Mary.

Frances Fields

Californian, born, raised and educated. Graduated from St. Mary's Hospital School of Nursing and worked in the OR for many years. Was married, had two children, and lived in Napa. Her husband was appointed to the US Foreign Service and they traveled extensively, living abroad for many years. She has been writing since joining the Foreign Service in 1967. Letters home were the only way to stay in contact with family and friends from remote outposts. Later she returned to school for her B.A. in Nursing Administration. Subsequently she owned and operated a Bed and Breakfast for seven years. She is currently retired.

Nancy Freeman

Nancy graduated from the California College of Arts & Crafts in Oakland. Her portfolio includes advertising, textbook illustrations, greeting cards, and commissioned art quilts. In 2012 Nancy was invited to join a small group of writers in Benicia. She politely declined, saying she'd never written anything other than the occasional e-mail. Later, she relented, and memories of less-than-ideal travel companions, quirky acquaintances, and boyfriends bubbled to the surface. She now has quite a collection of memoirs. *Shy* is Nancy's debut into the glittering scene of publishing.

Deborah Fruchey

Deborah Fruchey is the author of five books and the editor of another five. Her own books include poetry, comedy romance, self-help, and flash fiction. Her first novel was chosen as a Best Book by the American Bookseller's Association in 1987. A second poetry book, *Three Kinds of Dark,* is due out this year from Zeitgeist Press. Visit Deborah at www.lafruche.net and find her books on Smashwords and Amazon.

Carol Gieg

Carol Gieg's memoir, *TBI-to Be Injured, Surviving and Thriving after a Brain Injury*, is written from an insider's point-of-view. She suffered a traumatic brain injury, followed by neurosurgery, yet survived and is thriving. She combines her own experience, as well as research done in the field of traumatic brain injury, to encourage other victims. Specific exercises are offered to improve what is possible and to compensate for what is not. Carol's poems and prose pieces have been featured in anthologies, periodicals, and other venues. She lives in Benicia, California, with her husband.

Beth Grimm

Beth Grimm lives in Benicia. For thirty years she was a condo-minium lawyer and mediator. In her career she published over forty books, primers, and many articles.

Since her retirement, road tripping around the US has brought her a host of new experiences. She spent six years capturing the sarcastic humorous moments her father offered as her peculiar muse. Her book, *The Great Grandpa Chronicles*, will be published by the summer of 2020. In addition to writing, she has found her stride teaching iPhone artistry.

Marty Malin, author and editor

Marty Malin began writing fiction after he retired and wishes he had begun sooner. He is the author of a collection of short stories, *Grandmother's Devil & Other Tempting Tales.* His fiction and poetry have been published online and in literary journals. He is active in the Benicia Writers Workshop and the Napa Valley Chapter of the California Writers Club. He hosts a monthly radio program, "The Storytellers," on KZCT FM Vallejo and is currently writing a novel.

Bruce Moody

If you enjoyed "The Jaunt," watch for *Water, a story in stories*—to be published in 2020 by Benicia Literary Arts—whose tales narrate the life of a man from boyhood to old age.

Bruce Moody's prize-winning work has appeared in *The New Yorker, Michigan Quarterly, The National Lampoon,* and elsewhere. *Roadside: Will Work For Food or $* is a memoir of his adventures as a roadside beggar. His papers are collected at The Boston University Library.

Aletheia Morden

Aletheia was born in England, lived in Los Angeles, and received degrees from Immaculate Heart College and Cal State. She's co-written screenplays and stage plays, tutored homeless children, been a paralegal, a member of the Billy the Kid Outlaw Gang, Inc., in New Mexico, an inner-city schools volunteer—having NASA's spacemobile visit was fun—reviewed movies for underground newspapers, body-surfed daily at age fifty, and has driven across America and Canada. Motto: Life's an adventure.

Deborah Morrison

Deborah Morrison has been a garden designer, beekeeper, special education teacher, wife, mother, daughter, sister, aunt, and friend. The seeds of her stories come from time spent in these roles. She is blessed with a loving husband, son, daughter, family, and friends who have all supported her and filled her life with joy and many happy memories. She is truly grateful for them all. She lives in Benicia with her husband of 41 years and a Silken Windhound named Keara.

Carolyn Plath

Carolyn Plath is a life-long writer, first receiving recognition for her work in 5th grade. "Think Dream Play," her weekly slice of life/humor column, ran in *The Benicia Herald* for five years, as did her advice column based on readers' submissions of their nightly dreams. Called "Send Me Your Dreams," it also appeared in the *Examiner.com*. Her movie reviews can be found on her blog *Cinema Cat* at www.cinemacat-tdp.blogspot.com.

Lois Requist, author and editor

Lois Requist received her B.A. and M.A. in English/Creative Writing from San Francisco State University. Her three published books are *Where Lilacs Bloom*; *RVing Solo Across America, without a cat, dog, man, or gun*; and *Late Harvest Green*, which was a finalist in two categories for the 2019 Next Generation Indie Book Awards. In addition, many of her short stories, poems, articles, and columns have been published. Poet Laureate of Benicia from 2012 to 2014 and founder of Benicia Literary Arts, she continues to be active in the literary community.

Rob Rogers

Rob Rogers is a writer, teacher, and journalist who works with 11th- and 12th-grade students at De La Salle High School in Concord and lives in Benicia, California.

When I'm not nattering on about transcendentalism, the American Dream, or slam poetry, you can generally find me puttering in the garden, learning to play harmonica, practicing archery, or playing heroes and villains with my five- and eight-year-old sons. I also like tea.

Nicky Ruxton

Nicky Ruxton pens fiction spotlighting itchy characters that need to scratch. Her first series of stories stuffed unrelated people into claustrophobic elevators, while another series confronts global rituals levied against women in the name of beauty. Her current work explores compulsions that drive her character's behavior without apology. She says of her work, "I open up a can of worms and make worm soup."

Irene Sardanis

Irene Sardanis is a retired psychologist. She was born in New York City to Greek immigrant parents. Independent Press Awards recently gave her *Out of the Bronx, a Memoir*, Best Inspirational book for 2020.

She has attended writing conferences in San Miguel de Allende; Mendocino, California; Key West, Florida; and Catamaran Writers Conference in Pebble Beach, California. She has also taken writing classes with Laura Davis, Charlotte Cook, and Mark Greenside. She resides in Oakland, California, with her wonderful husband, John.

Stephen Schelling

Stephen Schelling is a writer, teacher, pickler, and an Eagle Scout from America with a B.A. in journalism from Marshall University. Originally from the Washington D.C. area, he wrote professionally for the West Virginia State Legislature and freelanced in Southern California and South Korea. Now, he teaches English Language Arts at Vallejo High School, often on his roller blades while playing his guitar. He writes in the genres of realistic literary fiction, horror, and postmodernism.

Marilyn Tavlin

After her father's premature death in Oklahoma, Marilyn grew up in her mother's hometown of New Orleans. Her mother remarried, and the family grew to include nine children. The household was chaotic; the adults overwhelmed. Marilyn married at 17, and produced two unique, talented children. In 1994 she moved to Los Angeles, where she lived for 15 years and began her writing studies. Marilyn retired in 2017 after 50 years in the legal field. She now writes, and is currently working on her memoir. Marilyn lives in Vallejo with her cat Buster.

Teresa Van Woy

Dr. Teresa Van Woy lives in Benicia, California, with her husband and three daughters. She is a board-certified podiatrist with a passion for world travel, backpacking, photography, martial arts, and woodworking. She is currently working on her memoir titled: *Wildflower, A Tale of Transcendence: From Abuse and Poverty to Flourishing Physician.*

Becky Bishop White

Becky Bishop White, a Benicia resident, feels the pull of the Carquinez Strait's tidal waters to create something—anything—virtually every day. An award-winning, published poet, Becky occasionally writes prose. Her spooky story, "The Party," originated as a narrated piece for Halloween on The Storytellers, a regular segment of Art Beat on Vallejo public radio KZCT.

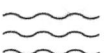

Editors

James White, Benicia Literary Arts President, editor

Jim is a California-based writer of historical, literary, and science fiction. He earned an M.A. in U.S. History. His professional career has included military service, teaching, working as a research librarian, and technical writing. Jim is currently serving as President of his town's literary society, Benicia Literary Arts. Jim's stories have appeared in *Datura Literary Journal*, *The Wapshott Press*, *Remington Review*, and *Adelaide Books*. His third novella, *Carp Cafe* launches later in 2020 through Black Opal Books.

Mary Eichbauer, Editor-in-Chief, Benicia Literary Arts

Born in New York City, Mary Eichbauer graduated in the first class of women at Caltech. She holds an M.A. and Ph.D. in Comparative Literature from UCLA, and taught Humanities, English Literature, and Women's Studies. She serves on the Benicia Library Board of Trustees, and the boards of Vallejo Symphony, Friends of the Benicia Library, and Benicia Literary Arts. In times of no quarantine, she plays violin in the Solano Symphony. Her book of poetry, *After the Opera*, is available from Random Lane Press.

Marty Malin, author and editor

Marty Malin began writing fiction after he retired and wishes he had begun sooner. He is the author of a collection of short stories, *Grandmother's Devil & Other Tempting Tales.* His fiction and poetry have been published online and in literary journals. He is active in the Benicia Writers Workshop and the Napa Valley Chapter of the California Writers Club. He hosts a monthly radio program, "The Storytellers," on KZCT FM Vallejo and is currently writing a novel.

Lois Requist, author and editor

Lois Requist received her B.A. and M.A. in English/Creative Writing from San Francisco State University. Her three published books are *Where Lilacs Bloom*; *RVing Solo Across America, without a cat, dog, man, or gun*; and *Late Harvest Green*, which was a finalist in two categories for the 2019 Next Generation Indie Book Awards. In addition, many of her short stories, poems, articles, and columns have been published. Poet Laureate of Benicia from 2012 to 2014 and founder of Benicia Literary Arts, she continues to be active in the literary community.

Gallery

Merrilee Cavenecia   Judea Cavoto   Grant Cooke   Mary Eichbauer

Tamar Enoch   Frances Fields   Nancy Freeman   Deborah Fruchey

Carol Gieg   Beth Grimm   Marty Malin   Bruce Moody

Aletheia Morden

Deborah Morrison

Carolyn Plath

Lois Requist

Rob Rogers

Nicky Ruxton

Irene Sardanis

Stephen Schelling

Marilyn Tavlin

Teresa Van Woy

Becky Bishop White

James W. White

Acknowledgements

Since Benicia Literary Arts incorporated in 2012, we have wanted to produce another volume of the *Carquinez Review*. The name "Carquinez" refers to the Carquinez Strait, a narrow channel of fresh water from the Sierras that mixes with saltwater from the San Francisco Bay, connecting us to the larger Bay Area and beyond.

When we set about to produce this book, we first solicited manuscripts of short stories. These submissions were blind reviewed by a selection panel that included:

Ann Kamoe, a travel agent and lifelong editor with a background in newspaper journalism.

Ken MacLennan, curator at the Pleasanton Museum and the author of *Pleasanton, California: A Brief History*.

Kristine Mietzner, whose prose has appeared in many literary journals and local newspapers. Her forthcoming novel *Matisse in Winter* was a finalist in the San Francisco Writers Conference Writing Contest.

Toni Morgan, author of six novels and a National Book Award in Literature nominee for *Queenie's Place*, as well as a new collection of short stories *Between Love and Hate*.

Bob Stanley, editor of two poetry anthologies who has published three collections of his own work and served as Poet Laureate of Sacramento City and County from 2009 to 2012

With the recommendations from these reviewers, the editorial staff worked individually with each of the selected authors. The editorial staff included James W. White, Project Editor; Mary Eichbauer, Editor-in-Chief, Benicia Literary Arts; and editors Lois Requist and Marty Malin.

The cover photograph was provided by Beth Grimm.

Jan Malin of Canyon Rose Press was the book designer.

All of these folks worked together on the many decisions that went into producing this volume. To everyone who made the new *Carquinez Review* a reality, a big thank you!

James W. White
Project Editor, *Carquinez Review*

Le Monde Livre, the typeface used in this book, was designed by the French type designer Jean François Porchez in 1999. He is one of the pioneers of digital typography and his typefaces have won numerous prizes. (As an added tidbit, Le Monde Livre is used by France's President Macron for his official correspondence.)

www.ingramcontent.com/pod-product-compliance
Lightning Source LLC
Chambersburg PA
CBHW071559110726
47908CB00007B/2169